DARK FAE

CELTIC LEGACY BOOK3

SHANNON MAYER

HIJINKS INK PUBLISHING

Dark Fae

Celtic Legacy Book III

Shannon Mayer

Copyright © 2012 Shannon Mayer

Electronic Edition

To know more about Shannon Mayer, please visit her blog:

http://shannonmayer.blogspot.com

 Created with Vellum

Dark Fae

Celtic Legacy Book III

Shannon Mayer

Copyright © 2012 Shannon Mayer

Electronic Edition

To know more about Shannon Mayer, please visit her website:

www.shannonmayer.com

Cover Art: Damonza

✳ Created with Vellum

ACKNOWLEDGMENTS

As always, I couldn't have made these pages sing
without my amazing team of editors, Melissa
Breau and Rachel Peterson who worked overtime
to help me get "Dark Fae" out to the readers.
To my amazing husband for his support and love,
and his belief in me and my writing.
And to my readers. Your reviews, emails, tweets
and Facebook messages truly keep me going on
the tough days when my muse wanders away.

1

"Who so loves believes the impossible."
Elizabeth Barrett Browning

The wind whipped around the lake edge, far colder than it should have been for the summer months here on Vancouver Island. Or maybe it was just the chill in my soul I was feeling so keenly. I shivered and wrapped my arms around my upper body and held on tight.

My mind kept going back to the hardest truth I'd ever been handed. My little sister had been taken over by the entity known as Chaos, and there was no way to get her back.

I'd lost her for good this time. Not to the Fomorii below the waves. Not to Balor. Not to some stupid prophecy, but to Chaos.

A voice cut through the pain, deep and resonate with Irish brogue.

"I'm sorry. Quinn, please believe me that I thought I was doing what was best for Ashling. I was doing all I could to keep her safe."

I kept my back to Bres, unwilling to look him in the eye or even bother to give him an answer. How could he think he could possibly know what was best for Ashling? She was my sister first and I'd been looking after her for my entire life. I'd been the one to chase away her nightmares, to sit at the table after school and help her with her homework, and to comfort her on Darcy's—our neglectful mother—bad days. Bres had only *just* found out she was his half-sister; there was no way he could possibly care for her as much as I did. Nor could he understand what it was doing to me to stand there and do nothing.

Bres and I stood waiting on the edge of the banshee queen's bower while Fianna attended to Luke. He'd been badly injured, and Fianna had agreed to help him heal. But she'd also said it wasn't a guarantee. Luke might not make it.

My hands clenched, along with my stomach and that same chill wind whipped through my heart. It seemed everyone around me was doomed to some horrible death or suffering, and the guilt sat heavily on me, making me feel as though I was a plague on those I loved.

The worst part was that I couldn't save Ashling or Luke, and there was nothing I could do to heal the wounds I was causing by being the "Chosen One" that some prophecy of the fae said I was.

I didn't have the ability to heal injuries that Ashling did. Glancing at the entryway to the bower, I was grabbed by another twist of fear that this was taking too long. Luke, as one of the Tuatha should have healed faster than any human, even with grievous injuries. But the last view I'd had of Luke was one that left little doubt as to the deadliness of the banshee poison coursing through his system. His blue eyes had been dull, barely gray, his cheeks sunken, and he'd had skin the shade of bread dough.

I wished Lir—the father I'd only just met—was with us still.

But he had gone, and left me alone with Bres and all those feelings swirling between us. I understood that Lir had a job to do, responsibilities that required his attention, and I knew that he'd had to leave. He would make an attempt to wake the old gods to face Chaos, and that in and of itself was no small task; it had to be done or at least he had to try.

That didn't mean I wasn't still wishing Lir was at my side instead of Bres.

At the very least, his presence would take the strain off me in trying to ignore Bres while secretly wanting to throttle him.

Or kiss him. I frowned at that wayward thought that caught me off guard. No, I did not want to kiss Bres.

The simple fact was that I'd spent a lifetime yearning for a father, only to meet him and have to say goodbye within an hour of laying eyes on each other. For the first time in my life, I had a parent who cared for me and yet I couldn't even have him with me.

"You going to ignore me for the rest of your life?" Bres asked. "Quinn, you have to know I be beating myself up over Ashling. I shoulda seen what was happening, and I didn't."

I snapped off a branch of huckleberries, the tiny red fruit vibrant against the all-green bush. Plucking them off one at a time, I popped them in my mouth as if I had nothing better in the world to do.

"I'm busy, leave me alone," I said between bites of the tart, red fruit. Childish? You bet, but I just didn't trust myself around him.

"Quinn, look at me." His Irish brogue was more than a little tempting, and my body swayed toward his voice. Damn it, I hated that the sound of him drew me in. I glanced over my shoulder.

"You made yourself very clear before about what you thought of me, of what you thought me capable of." I couldn't stop the flush that lit my face. No doubt I was bright red. Without knowing what I'd been doing, I had called Bres in a dream, and all but threw myself at him. To be fair, I thought he had feelings for me, but after what he'd said, I knew I'd only been fooling myself.

His words reverberated through my head.

I can't save you both.

It's Ashling or you.

You'll kill her.

Bres's lips tightened and he looked straight up into the treetops, the muscles in his neck flexing. As he spoke, he looked away from the trees and back to me. "I said those things because of what I saw in a vision, what I know now Chaos showed me. I saw the battle between you and Ashling. I saw you take her head. I know it was in the future, but I didn't want to believe you could do it but . . .that's why I said what I said. How could I protect her from you if I . . ." He shook his head.

Anger, hurt, grief and more anger flared. "If you what?" I walked toward him, feeling my power rise under my skin, my magic reacting to my emotions. "You thought you'd treat me like crap and that would make it easier for you to fight me? You thought that if you beat me down with your words, I wouldn't be able to stand against you?" He opened his mouth but I cut him off, not giving him a chance to deny what he'd done. "You thought I would be able to kill her? That I have it in me to kill my baby sister? Yeah, awesome. You know what? It just goes to show how well you know me, and how well you know her. Ashling *knows* I won't hurt her. It's the rest of the world that's trying to kill us, not each other."

Bres didn't back up as I'd advanced on him, which meant I ended up toe-to-toe with him and looking up into his violet eyes. "You know, you had a lot to say before when you wanted to tell me that I would do the unthinkable." I said, "You have nothing to say now?"

I expected anger and defiance out of him, not the softening of his lips and eyes with a heavy sorrow that I could almost feel.

He lifted his hand and put the tips of his fingers to the edge of my jaw. "I was wrong, even though I thought I was protecting her. Chaos has fooled us all, Balor, me and . . . she has cost me more than my little sister. She cost me my chance with the one person I wanted the most." His voice lowered, and with it, his head as if he was going to kiss me.

I didn't even think about it, my body reacted faster than ever before. Which meant the slap seemed to surprise us both. His head snapped to the side, a trickle of blood from the corner of his mouth spraying out. My hand stung, tingling all over.

You have to remember that you are stronger now, Quinn. Cora whispered to me from the back of my mind. My grandmother had been a five-foot-long snake when we'd met because of a curse. She'd died protecting me. Then I'd almost died, and when I'd come back from the other side, it was with her as my guide. The whole relationship was weird, but it worked and her mentorship was all that had kept me going at times.

He probably is sorry. She said. *One thing Bres has always been is honest.*

"He probably should be sorry," I said under my breath. The whisper of bushes being parted and the low hum of voices pulled my attention around.

Fianna, the banshee queen, stood across from me, her long white hair floating on some unseen breeze as her deep, soulful, brown eyes, as wide as any deer's, looked us up and down as if sensing the tension of the previous moment. I pulled myself together and walked away from Bres.

"How is he? How is Luke?" I asked.

She shook her head. "He has a very short time left. The poison is different than the banshee poison you were infected with. Aednat was very old, very powerful. The toxin from her bite is beyond fierce and even Lugh's strength is not enough to counteract it."

"Can't we call someone? Someone who can heal? Ashling healed me through the mirror. We could do the same for Luke," I said, already wondering where the closest mirror might be. There had to be a way to help him.

"It is not so simple, Quinn." She spread her hands in front of her, the spider web woven skirt she wore billowing with the slight movement.

"This poison he carries within him, you cannot heal. We can only make him comfortable until the end. I am sorry for your loss."

Her words didn't really register. Not right away. Because it wasn't possible that Luke wouldn't get better. He was my friend and maybe even something more, something or someone I was only just beginning to appreciate. He loved me more than I loved him, but I had been trying to catch up, had thought I would have time to.

Without him, how would we convince Nuadha and the Tuatha to help me stand against Balor? I needed him here with me to help save Ashling, to help get us all out of this mess. There was no way the council with Nuadha at the helm would trust Bres now that he'd defected back to his father. And I was an interloper, which meant there was no way that I was going to be trusted.

Luke was the key to making that happen.

Bres's hands rested on my shoulders from behind. I wanted to fling them off, but I suddenly had no strength in me. I struggled to find the right words. Because I had to make sure I wasn't jumping to conclusions.

"Fianna, I don't understand. What do you mean we just make him comfortable until the end?

You can't mean . . ." My mind refused to see what she was saying, balked at the truth they were trying to show me.

You know what she is saying, Luke is – I blocked out Cora. Shut her down before those words slipped through my mind.

Fianna stepped forward her eyes as gentle as her words. "You should go see him before it is too late." She motioned for me to step through into her bower, the woven branches of trees and vines creating a cathedral made with every aspect of the forest.

As if in a dream, I stepped forward, her words settling on me like weights wrapping around my neck, squeezing the air out of me. Everything around me slowed: my movements, the pressure of the wind, the birds and the sounds of the forest.

Step, step, step. I was into the bower now and in the center on a bed of moss lay Luke.

My eyes focused on him and I struggled to swallow, my throat tight. His eyes were closed and his skin was nearly gray in color, as if he'd already passed over. I stood and waited for him to breathe, counting the seconds. I started to panic when I got to thirty, then forty. I stumbled the last few steps to his side and dropped to my knees, and it was as if the impact of my body hitting the ground reminded him to draw breath. A deep, rattling, gurgling breath that smelled sour like poorly fermented wine and vomit.

I took his hands in mine, shocked at how cold they were. "Blankets, don't you have any blankets for him?" I asked, looking up to see Fianna and Bres staring down at me.

She shook her head. "Feel his face."

Laying his hands on his stomach, I slipped my hands up to his face, and quickly snatched them back. He was literally burning up, though he showed no sign of it anywhere else. His face was paler than before without a hint of color, that gray tinge spreading down his neck.

"There is nothing we can do now," Fianna said. "Soon his ancestors will come and guide him home to where he will be at peace, and without pain that this world gives so freely."

"That's not true," Bres said. "What about the cauldron? That could be the answer."

Fianna spun to face him, her skirt swirling outward, skimming across Luke's face. I wondered if he could feel or hear anything, I wondered if he knew he was dying. Or if he knew that this was all my fault.

Cora sighed. *Do not take his death on you, Quinn. He chose his path, as you chose yours. And as to whether or not he feels anything, I doubt it. Likely, he floats as you did between old memories.*

Fianna's voice was sharp, cutting overtop of Cora's words in my mind. "Do not fill her with false hope. The cauldron has been hidden away. No one has found it in years. Searching for it would be a waste of her time and energy when there is far more pressing matters for her to deal with."

Bres's voice was tight, clipped. "I say that you are wrong. The cauldron was always kept within the bounds of the Enchanted Forest in Ireland. Mayhap you don't want to be helping us. Maybe you be on the side of Chaos. Because Lugh here, if he dies would make it that much easier for Chaos to win."

Fianna and the banshees around us gasped and, in the silence that followed, Luke drew another rattling breath, the sound filling the tense air. Looking over my shoulder, I eyed Bres as he locked eyes with the banshee queen.

Standing there just behind me, Bres faced Fianna down. His eyes were hard, and his stance spoke volumes.

"Quinn needs Luke. He's her future. We have to

save him before we go after Chaos. There's no telling what will happen if Quinn tries to face her alone, without her man with her." He paused. "Not to mention he's the only one that Nuadha will trust enough to follow into a battle with Chaos." His words settled over me. Bres was fighting for me, though that meant I was to be with someone else. A dull aching throb started deep in my heart, but I ignored it, doing my best to push it away. His words echoed my earlier thoughts. We needed Luke for more than just my aching heart.

Fianna put her hands on her hips. She let out an exaggerated sigh. After several seconds of staring at Bres, her eyes narrowed, and she finally shrugged. "Fine, but if she fails and the world falls, it will be on your head, Bres. I can take you to the place that crosses over, but it could mean your death and hers. I do not want to be the one to end our singular hope that we will hold out against Chaos."

I clutched Luke's hands. His fingers were icy as if he'd been dunked in arctic water and then set in our freezer back home that kept the ice cream so hard, we couldn't scoop it out. I shook my head knowing the tangent my brain was running off to was an attempt to escape the truth. Luke was dying. Luke was dying and unless we did something soon, we were going to lose him.

I looked at Fianna, willing her to make eye contact with me. "I can't just let him die, not if there's a chance we could save him," I said. Guilt clawed at my guts despite what Cora had said earlier. It was my fault Luke was dying, just like it was my fault Ashling had been taken by the Fomorii in the first place. Maybe I couldn't save Ashling, but maybe I *could* save Luke.

Bres nodded his agreement. "We have to try."

Cora's voice came through loud and clear. *You don't have time or the luxury. You have other things you must do to save our world. Luke understands that. He wouldn't want you to put your life in danger for him.*

I didn't answer her. I just put Luke's hands back on his chest, and then stood and dusted my pants off. There was no longer any hesitation. I couldn't be afraid, not when the people I cared about were dying around me.

"Fianna, take us to the place we must go," I knew this was only the first step. We still had to find the three Smiths in the hope they could make a new Excalibur, a weapon that would be the death of my sister. No, not my sister, of Chaos.

Suppressing that thought, I steeled my resolve. Save Luke first, get the sword after. Don't think about the final step, not yet.

You are a fool, girl. Cora whispered.

I nodded, but didn't answer her. I didn't need to. Fool or not, I was doing this my way.

2

As we prepared to leave with Fianna and go to where we would seek out a cauldron that could save Luke's life, a willowy banshee that looked to be about twelve years old bolted into the queen's bower. She was shaking hard, and sweat dripped off the edge of her chin. Her eyes—a beautiful hazel—were huge and dilated. Fear radiated around her, infecting the other banshees in a matter of seconds. The entire group began to shift, distancing themselves from the messenger.

"Calling mirror, a powerful woman wishes to speak with you," she whispered, handing a silvered mirror to Fianna. I recognized it right away. The mirror was the same one Aednat had brought me to call Ashling on.

The thought of Aednat made me sick to my stomach. I'd killed her. Only a few short days ago, I'd been like any other twenty-two-year-old. I'd been on a weekend away with my little sister. How could it be in that time, I'd changed so much that not only was I capable of killing someone, but of killing Aednat, who reminded me so much of Ashling? I didn't have the answer to that question. I only knew that I was doing things that my past self would have been shocked to see come to life.

Aednat had brought out the protective side of me, but I had still killed her without hesitation when the moment had become clear that there was no other way. Me. I'd ended her life. Squinting my eyes shut, I took a deep breath, held it, and then let it out slowly. The world had spun on me, flipped my perception of it inside out, and I had to change in order to survive the shift. That didn't mean I was happy with that fact. I didn't have to like the new part of my life that included monsters and death.

Fianna accepted the mirror from the young messenger and swirled her hand around it. The silver-edged calling mirror slipped from her hand but didn't fall to the ground. Instead it hovered in midair, shimmering and bending as it flexed its borders. The mirror stretched until it was about two feet wide and nearly six feet tall, large enough for a person to see her entire outfit. Or, in this case, it was large enough for Ashling to be completely visible on the other side of it.

"Ash!" I shouted, starting forward in excitement. She had perfect timing. I'd broken through the mirror once, which had allowed Ashling to heal me. I knew she could do it again for Luke. "Ash, you have to help Luke!"

"No, Quinn, it isn't her anymore," Bres said, the urgency and fear that laced his voice stopping me. "Look at her, really *look* at her."

I stopped where I was and did as he asked. She had the same strawberry blond curls, the same petite figure, shape of her mouth and face where the same, the same eyes . . . no, that was the difference. Her eyes, once the color of new spring grass had darkened to the green of mold and damp things, nearly black in places. Things shuffled and shimmered in those now darkened irises. Her head remained halfcocked to the right, as if she was listening to music only she could hear. She stepped forward, her joints jerking and popping as if she were a marionette rather than a living being. I couldn't stop myself from stepping back. I knew that mirror could be passed through. I'd done it myself.

"I don't think this is a good idea," I said.

Ashling sneered at me, lips rippling up over her teeth as she spoke with a voice that was hers, and yet not. Darker, and full of anger. "You should listen to Balor's weakest link. He is actually helping you stay alive, which is more than he could do for your little sister." Her voice was heavy and thick, as though she spoke underwater and I was only hearing the echo of it. She snickered. "For now. Soon this world will be mine as it should have been from the start. Chaos will reign for all time."

Ashling's voice and words wreaked havoc on my heart. Lir had been right. He'd told me before he'd left that seeking out Ashling would end the only chance we had at stopping Chaos. Seeing her now, I knew in my heart that he was speaking the truth. Ashling was gone, there was nothing left of her. Chaos had her body and was using it as her own.

It felt as though my heart cracked inside my chest, shattering like a piece of glass.

Fianna stepped up to the mirror. "Why have

you called us, Chaos? What purpose is this uncalled for visit?"

Ashling, Chaos now, began to pace in front of the mirror with that odd jerking movement as though she weren't quite sure how to move her body. "I want you to do something for me, Banshee Queen." Her eyes flickered to mine, those dark shadows behind them made my skin crawl.

"What is that you would ask of us, but more importantly, what would you give us in return?" Fianna said, clasping her hands in front of her body.

Chaos flung one hand toward me and I flinched. "That one is prophesied to end my life. I doubt she has it in her to complete the task, not with all the love she has for her baby sister." She laughed, her mouth opening so wide the skin at the edge of her lips stretched to the point of splitting.

My spine stiffened and I squared my shoulders. No point in denying that, at least, a portion of what she said was true. As soon as we got Luke healed, I refused to believe there was any other option. I was going to do all I could to stop Chaos. She'd stolen Ashling's life, I wouldn't let her steal anyone else's.

Fianna turned and lifted a brow at me,

assessing me. "I can see she has already decided to end your life, to stop you if she is able. I see in her eyes that she knows her sister is gone, and that you are the enemy now."

The air around us shifted, becoming far cooler than any summer air should be. Bres stepped up beside me and bent his head to my ear. "This is about to get bad. Be ready."

Chaos snapped her fingers and the entire screen filled with half her face, that strange shifting within her eyes mesmerizing me. "You, Banshee Queen, will receive everything you always wanted if you do one small thing for me. You will rule this Dark Isle with no interference from the Tuatha or Fomorii. I will leave you and your people in peace."

The only sound was Fianna's skirts, swishing as she walked toward the mirror. "For what task will I receive these honors that you would hand me?"

Chaos smiled, a half smile on the mirror, and a parody of Ashling's beauty rippling over her skin. "You will kill that one." She dipped her head toward me. No surprise there. But what shocked me was that Fianna didn't say she wouldn't. My gut tightened and my muscles tensed. Chaos went on. "A little task, easy for you and your banshees.

Already, one of her protectors is dying and the other, well, he could prove a fun aside for you and your . . . ladies. A powerful line of banshees could come from him."

Bowing her head, chin to her chest, Fianna seemed to be thinking over the request. Was she insane?

"You can't!" I burst out, unable to contain the words. "You can't possibly trust this creature! You know that she won't keep her word!" Even as the words escaped my mouth, I cringed. Creature. Was that all Ashling was to me now? Yes, the truth was right there in front of me.

"SILENCE!" Fianna roared. "Restrain her."

Ah, shit.

The banshees swarmed toward us with the speed of a rushing wind. Before I could do more than draw my dagger, never mind cast a barrier they closed in all around us. Bres gave me a sharp shove and pushed me ahead of him and we ran, barely making it out of the bower before banshees closed ranks around us, far too many to fight and survive. Even I could see that.

Shit, shit, shit!

"Hold!" Fianna commanded and we all froze outside the bower, away from the mirror. I could just see the single eye, a small speck in the corner of what had once been Ashling's brilliant green orbs was all that was left. It was already hard to think of her as Ashling. This was what the prophecy was about: I wouldn't truly be killing Ashling. I'd be killing Chaos, that is, if we were able to get out of this current bind.

Bres bumped his hip against me. "Call to Ashling."

I tipped my head up to look at him. "What?"

"Call her, see if you can get her to respond. Maybe there's a small chance she's still in there." He made a slight motion with one hand and the banshees around us growled.

My heart thumped, pain coursing through it instead of blood, of that I was certain. "And if she can't hear me?"

Bres lowered his head, a single tear dripping from one eye. "Then I'll help you kill her."

3

Surrounded by banshees with Chaos calling for my head on a pike, I wasn't sure that I would get out of this current situation. But to have Bres tell me there was a chance that Ashling was still inside of her body, trapped with Chaos . . .how could I deny trying to bring her forward?

My throat tightened to the point of closing off the words that wanted to spill up and out. Bres curled his fingers around mine and tried to pull me into a half hug, but I pulled away.

"I tried to stop them, Quinn. But I wasn't strong enough on my own." Bres's voice broke on the last word. "I couldn't stop me own father from doing this, but I did try."

I didn't bother to hide the tears that slid down my cheeks. He'd tried to protect her, even from me, even from Balor, and I couldn't fault him for that, much as I wanted to. His actions toward me didn't mean he didn't love Ashling. Taking a deep breath, I nodded acknowledgement.

"Together then, we'll deal with Chaos if Ashling is lost." I squeezed his hand and then let him go.

With the banshees following in a loose semi-circle, we made our way back into the bower. Chaos had pulled back from the mirror so that her entire body showed once more. Hands on her hips, she tapped her foot while glowering at Fianna. "Answer me, Banshee queen, what do you say to my offer?"

Fianna lifted her head, but it was me who spoke first.

"Ashling! If you're still in there, you've got to fight with everything you have. You've got to fight! I won't give up on you!" I wanted to lay my hands on the mirror and pull her through, shake her till Chaos was thrown out.

Adrenaline raced through me, but there was nothing physical I could do. I couldn't fight this part for her. I couldn't even try to rescue her. I had no idea if it was even possible. "Ash, please, try," I said. "You're stronger than me, fearless in everything you've done in life. Please, try." I hoped that it would be enough that the strength of Ashling's heart would help her fight off Chaos.

The seconds ticked by, and nothing happened. There was no change in Chaos's eye, no glimmer of the little sister I'd tried to protect at all costs. I'd hoped Bres had been right, that there was some small piece of Ashling left, that we could help her be free of the evil that had taken over her body and bring her back to us.

Chaos threw back her head and laughed, the sound ripping through the air with a force that caused me to stumble to one knee. "You think to call your little sister? Fool, she buckled under me in minutes, she is not strong. She is weak, just like you. But go ahead, call her again if you want. It amuses me." She winked at me. I shook my head. There was nothing I could do or say to bring Ashling back, and it killed me to admit that even to myself. I dug my hands into the mossy ground, the cold damp earth grounding me.

It is all you can do, Quinn. You must let her go. Her soul will move on when she finally gives up fighting Chaos. She will go to that place where you went, she will go to her ancestors and be safe and at peace. Cora's words didn't exactly soothe me.

Chaos snorted and waved at us. "Kill them or die yourself. If you do not do as I ask, I will sink this island just like the last place that defied me, *Queen.*" She snarled the last word.

Fianna drew herself up. "I do not believe that you will honor what you say you will do. So, I will stand by the one who was chosen to defeat you long ago, I have faith in the strength of her heart."

Relief coursed through me. At least we hadn't lost our one ally.

Fianna clapped her hands and the mirror began to shrink. Chaos flipped her head back and bared her teeth at us. "So be it." She paused and her eyes narrowed, but it was me she stared down, not Fianna. "You will regret this moment. I will make you wish the banshees had finished you off and died in a toxin induced stupor."

In a blinding flash of light the mirror exploded, shards flying every which way. Bres tackled me to the ground, a barrier springing up around us. The ringing of glass bouncing off the barrier would have been almost pretty if it weren't for the fact it was interspersed with the cries of the banshees around us.

I made a move to get up, but Bres held me to the ground. "Let the last of the shards fall."

My face was buried in his neck, his hair tickling my nose and I made a mistake of taking a deep breath. Our bodies were flush against each other, held down by the barrier, but that deep breath pushed us even closer together. My eyes flew to his as the violet irises disappeared under the instant flush of heat, his pupils dilating with desire. I tried to focus on what Luke had told me. Bres had used his charm on me which was why I was feeling this way. Knowing that didn't really help as much as I'd hoped.

"Off," I said, scrambling to push him off. "Get off me." All I succeeded in was tangling our limbs more as I rolled us so that I was on top. Nope, that was not better. "Bres, let the barrier down!"

His Adam's apple dipped, and he gave a nod. The barrier dropped, and I leapt off him. Everywhere he'd touched me was as if I'd been scorched, my skin tingled, the intensity of that brief contact cutting straight through me.

"Damn it," I muttered to myself.

Shake it off, Quinn. It was only a moment. Cora said.

I sent my thoughts back to her rapid fire. *The*

last thing I need right now, Cora, is to have you make comments about awkward moments.

That wasn't awkward. That was unresolved passion that you don't want to acknowledge.

My eyes popped open wide and I couldn't stop the gasp that slipped past my lips.

You can try to deny it, but it was there from the beginning. Luke believes he loves you, of course, but Bres has cared for you not because of any prophecy demanding he must...

"Shut up!" I shouted and the world around me went still. Fianna stared at me. Her eyebrows lifted, a cut dripping blood down the side of her face. The rest of the banshees froze and I didn't dare turn to look at Bres.

"Quinn, do you be all right?" Bres asked, his brogue rolling over me, reminding me how good it felt to be against his hard body. How safe I was in his arms.

I ignored him. It was the only thing I could do. To Cora, I added, *That was charm, nothing else! Bres charmed me and I fell for it.* I closed her out of my thoughts and turned back to the queen. "My apologies, Fianna. Please, you were going to take us somewhere to find the cauldron. Let's continue."

Her brows were still high, but she placed her hands together and gave me a nod. "Of course. It is deep in the forest. We will speak of what will come as we walk."

Raising one elegant hand, she beckoned for Bres and me to follow her. I jogged to catch up to her, making sure to keep Bres out of my line of vision.

"Can we go faster?" I asked, thinking of Luke lying there, his life slipping away from him.

Fianna paused. "If you wish to go faster we can, but you will not be prepared to face the choice if you are taken there too swiftly."

Bres walked a few steps behind us, and while he hadn't said a word, every part of me was aware of him, my skin tingling still from being so close to him. Damn it, this was the last thing I needed right now.

I gritted my teeth. I was meant to be with Luke. That's what the prophecy said and so far, the bloody thing had been right, down to me having to kill my little sister. My guts churned on that and I pushed that horror away. One step at a time.

I stumbled and Bres reached out and steadied me, a flush of heat rolling between us again. Just from a hand on my back.

I told myself that just because I was attracted to Bres did not mean I loved him. Love took time, it wasn't instant.

First thing first, I had to help Luke. There was no other choice. If I couldn't save even a single person, how would I save the whole world? Admitting I was afraid was not an option anymore, not with the number of people depending on me to somehow find a way to kill Chaos. So what choice was there? I felt in my heart that Luke was needed, if not for me then for the Tuatha. The prophecy said he was to be at my side, or at least one version of the prophecy said he was to be at my side. This was a side journey I had to take, no matter what anyone else thought.

Fianna paused at the edge of a tree line I hadn't even noticed. "Here begins the swamp. It is deep within this land that we will find out if your destiny brings you here, or some foolish desire to save one who is meant to die. One life for many, that is often a choice heroes must make, Quinn. I pray to the old gods that you are choosing with not only your heart, but your head as well."

Before I could come up with any snappy response, she continued to speak, stepping into the swamp and sinking up over her knees in the murky, vegetation filled water.

"What you seek in this place is the cauldron. It is the one relic of the past that can save Luke. Within it is the power to heal all wounds, and at one time, it could even bring back the dead restoring them to their full life."

I sloshed into the swamp, the tepid water and murk hiding God only knew what. "If that's true, why hasn't it been found already?"

Bres answered me. "Because it is hidden, not only by conventional means, but by your own heart. It be a powerful relic and one that should not be used lightly."

That didn't make any sense, how could something be hidden by your own heart? Fianna half turned to look at us both. "Bres speaks truly. You must be honest within your heart for the reasons you seek out the cauldron. A single lie and you will disappear into the fog of the gateways forever, never to return to the land of the living."

Her words didn't really have time to register. Gateways and fog, and being honest were all jumbling up in my head as something shifted in the water ahead of us.

Something long, sinuous, and fast if the ripples were any indication.

Fianna lifted her hand, and crooned softly. But the creature shot past her and headed straight for me. In the brief seconds before it attacked, all I could take in was the sheer size of the thick body, and the green and black pattern on the diamond shaped two-foot-wide head. This was *not* a natural predator here on the island, not even close.

Knee deep in the muck, I didn't have a lot of room to maneuver. I called my dagger to my hand and met the open-fanged snake as it struck. It lunged at me, extended fangs dripping with venom. The dagger caught the top edge of its mouth and it hissed, curling away from me, its black eyes glittering.

"I cannot command this creature," Fianna said. "It is already under another's control."

There was a quick flash of gold in its irises and I knew what or rather who I was dealing with—my half-brother Card. It wasn't the first time he'd attacked me using an animal as a weapon.

"Quinn, back away!" Bres shouted, charging forward. I didn't have the luxury of waiting for him.

Again the snake struck at me, and again I

managed to dodge the bite that I had no doubt would prove to be far more painful than the sting of Cora's fangs.

When it lifts its head to strike, the throat is exposed. Cora's words distracted me, and I stumbled back, the water sloshing over my body as a coil from the snake wrapped around my legs, jerking me under. Even though I knew I wouldn't drown, something kept me from opening my mouth in the darkness that closed over my head.

Twisted upside down, I couldn't have found the surface if I'd been loose of the snake's coils.

Card's voice whispered through the water. "Your death is assured."

I managed to free one hand and flipped him off, even if he couldn't see me it was a small act of defiance. The coils tightened and I grimaced, keeping my lips closed tight.

Clawing at the coils with one hand I fought to get my other hand free. My wrist holding the dagger was wrapped securely with a band of the muscular snake.

Other hand, I thought to myself, I need the dagger in my other hand.

There was a moment that I wasn't sure I could do it and then the blade handle was gone from my right hand, and my left hand held the dagger tight. Eyes open under the water I could barely make out the head of the snake from the dark waters. A ripple of hard flesh here and there, the only thing for certain were the coils that wrapped around me.

I slashed at the snake with my dagger, feeling the flesh part under the tip of my blade and the coils loosened. I floated to the surface and a hand grabbed my hair and pulled me to my feet. I wobbled, sucking wind hard as the water dripped off me.

"Already Chaos sends death our way," Fianna said as she steadied me on my feet.

"Not Chaos," I grunted. "Card."

There was a shout and the heavy thunk of blade meeting flesh. We spun around to see Bres standing over the now lifeless body of the massive snake, the head detached from the rest of the body. Dripping wet, he turned just his head to look over his shoulder, sword gripped in his hand. An image that made my already beating heart pick up more speed. "Quinn, you be alright? No bites?"

"Yes, I mean, no bites." That was about all I could manage. My mouth was dry, my heart pounding. It was the fight, just the fight that caused all this heart beating out of control business.

Fianna tugged on my hand. "Hurry, if the creatures here are no longer mine to command then none of us are safe. If you are right about the snake, then your brother is near, and that does not bode well for any of us."

Bres sloshed through the water to my side, asking the question I wanted to. "Why is it that you cannot control your own forest, Fianna?"

"Quinn burned my staff to ash. It held the key to controlling the forest. Without it, I can only control my banshees, and nothing more."

Right, there was *that* minor detail. "I didn't know that at the time. I was just trying to stay alive," I said, feeling the need to defend myself.

Fianna shrugged. "It is the path you walk now, taking Bres and me with you. The times of change are upon this world whether we like it or not."

With her words the swamp seemed to close in around us, blocking out the sun and sky. Even the sounds of the birds were muted under the low hanging branches and deep hanging moss.

"Quinn," Bres said.

I paused, waiting for him to catch up rather than look over my shoulder at him. I couldn't meet his eyes with my heart and hormones still trying to make me touch him. There was too much between us. For all that, we'd only known each other a short time, so much had happened that bound us together whether we wanted it or not.

"What is it?" I asked when he reached my side.

"Before we get there, I have to tell you something. I need to say it before I lose the chance," Bres said.

I was shaking my head before he finished speaking, still not willing to meet his eyes. "No need to confess. Luke told me that you'd charmed me back in the labyrinth. That it was a game to you."

The silence lasted for a split second. "WHAT?" He all but roared the word.

Cringing, I turned to face him. "It will wear off, right? Eventually?"

His eyes were wide and his jaw was hanging open. With a shiver that ran through his body, he seemed to wake up. Brushing past me, he changed the subject completely.

"There will be a choice when we get to where the cauldron is. Only one of us will be able to go through at a time."

"Fine, then I'll go through," I said, letting him

change the subject. I didn't want to rub it in that I knew he'd tricked me and that Luke had outed him on that game. The swamp reluctantly let go of my foot with a slurp as I stepped over a downed and rotting tree.

"No, Quinn, do you not hear what Fianna is saying? You could very well die if you go through the gateway, if that's *still* what you must step through?" He aimed the question at Fianna who lifted her hand, stopping us.

Ahead of us was the gateway to the cauldron. Or should I say, *gateways*.

4

Fianna had brought us to the entranceway wherein lay a cauldron that could save Luke's life. Only it wasn't a single gateway, but two.

Two large arbutus trees that were mirror images of each other stood waiting for us. One was the brilliant gleaming red skinned trunk that stood out even in this darkened swamp. The other tree, though the green leaves and twisted growth of the trunk were the same, was no gleaming red skinned tree. The trunk was blackened as if by a fire or bolt of lightning, only it glimmered with the same sheen as the first. Black skinned tree, that could not be a good thing.

Fianna pointed to the two trees with the sweep

of her hand, a move that would have made any gameshow host happy. "There lies your choice, Quinn. The gateway of gleaming bright represents the fae who have only good intentions, those who seek to do what is right, the ones who will give up their lives for the greater good even if it means they lose their lives." Shifting ever so slightly, she pointed to the blackened tree. "There lies the gateway for the dark fae. Those who have seen that which is good and turned away, those who would murder to achieve their goals, the ones who will only do what is best for themselves, forsaking the greater good."

My eyes flicked back and forth between the two trees. "And I have to choose what? The one that I think the cauldron is in?"

She shook her head. "No, you have to choose the one that you believe yourself to be. If you choose correctly, the cauldron will wait for you on the other side. If you choose incorrectly, you will die," she said.

Bres touched my forearm, the heat from his fingers made me jerk away from him. "That is why I should go, Quinn. I know what I am. I am one of the dark fae; there is no question in me that is who I am."

I shook my head, "No, that's not true. I know you." Even as the words slipped past my lips, the truth of them hit me. I knew him as if I'd known him my whole life. He was no dark fae, no matter that we were at times on opposite sides. Even if the bugger did charm me to make me kiss him.

Reaching out, I touched his hand, tentatively at first. "This is something I have to do. It is not on your shoulders, this is not for you to face. It isn't your fault that Luke is hurt so badly."

"If I go first, and fail, you still have a chance. You are the one the prophecy speaks of, and *if* it's right, you are the only one who can save us from Chaos." He brushed his fingers along my jaw, his eyes softening. "I'm doing this for you, Quinn. I'm sorry, please forgive me," he said as his hand dropped.

I didn't understand what he was about, not until it was already happening. He grabbed my hand, and then spun me around. Pushing me, he sent me into the deeper water, and I tripped over a submerged log, my body getting sucked under by the swamp. Fighting to reach the surface, I pushed off the mushy bottom.

"Bres!" I screamed his name, as I broke the water's surface, already knowing that I was too late. A flash of light and the dark gateway swallowed him whole. Damn him and his heroics!

I struggled forward, tangling once more in unseen roots under the mud slurry of water. Fianna stepped in front of me. "Give him a chance to be your hero, Quinn. It's what all men want. To prove themselves to the one they love."

She came to my side and helped me to my feet. The water and muck clung to me as if it were a second skin. "I've yet to decide if you are twice blessed or twice cursed," she said.

Wiping my face, flicking the mud off my fingers, I shivered. "What do you mean?"

"To be loved by not one, but two men of strength and heart. It is a blessing to have one, but two? I'm not so sure I'd want that even for myself. A hard choice will wait for you soon, if you survive all this death and Chaos." She stared at me, then cocked her head to one side, so like her little sister it gave me a chill.

"He doesn't love me. He charmed me," I said. The words sounded hollow even to my own ears.

Fianna laughed. "Bres is many things: warrior, guide, teacher, Fomorii, and Tuatha. But even I know he is not a charmer. It is the one thing that wasn't passed on to him by his father. Bres can't charm. It isn't one of his abilities."

I tried to tell you. Cora said softly.

The water dripped off the tip of my nose and chin. I was too stunned to even try to wipe it away. My brain couldn't handle this new information. No, I wasn't being honest. It was my heart that was struggling with it, not my mind.

"Come, let us stand on higher ground while we wait to see if Bres can find his way." Fianna led the way to a tree that was downed in some long-ago windstorm, but it was not submerged as so many of the others were. Climbing up, I stood with one hand braced on a branch that jutted up to the sky.

"The cauldron will test him to see if he is worthy to bring it back to the realm of the humans. It has not ventured out for many, many hundreds of years," she said.

I glanced at her, the white dress dry and unmarked as if we hadn't just sloshed through miles of swamp. "You say that like it's alive."

Fianna didn't look at me, but continued to stare at the two gateways. "It is. Like all objects of power, it lives and has a will of its own. Even Excalibur carried with it consciousness. It is how Arthur did so well in battle, they worked as a team rather than master and weapon." She said this as if everyone knew what she was talking about.

"How will we know if Bres . . ." I wanted to say lived or died, but I couldn't. I had a hard enough time thinking about Luke dying. I wasn't sure I could handle the thought of losing them both.

"One hour. If at the end of that time he has not emerged, it will then be your choice. I would ask you for the sake of our world to not go through with this." Now she did look at me, her brown eyes wide with her pleading. "You are our one chance at ending Chaos's reign before it begins in earnest. In that, Bres was correct. You must believe me when I say these two men of yours, no matter their love for you, are not worth throwing the world away for. Two lives for all the world is not a bargain to be made."

"I need Luke. I need him at my side if I'm to face down Chaos. It says so in the prophecy, and more than that, I feel it. Here." I put my hand over my heart. "I will do whatever it takes to save him, even if that means putting my own life in danger."

"And if you put the world at risk?"

I gripped a branch, the flaking bark crunching under my fingers. "If I need Luke to save the world, then I need to save him first. Period. I cannot save the world and stop Chaos without him." Or without Bres. My heart clenched and my belly tightened with fear. Damn it, hurry Bres. Hurry.

Silence reigned between us for some time after that the minutes ticking by, slow as molasses in February.

A thought had been rolling around inside my brain, ever since I'd faced down Aednat, and I broke the uneasy silence by changing the subject. "How could you face your sister knowing you'd have to kill her? How did you do it?"

She let out a sigh.

"We were not always enemies. I loved her more than anyone—I would have died for her even."

The words were so like my own when I spoke of Ashling, I wanted to put my hands to my ears and tell her to stop, but I had to hear this. I needed to find the strength to do what I had to do if I was going to face Ashling, even if it was just her body and no longer her heart and soul.

Fianna swirled her hand over the swampy water and a foggy image rose: a miniature picture of Aednat and Fianna. They were holding hands, walking along, smiling at one another. Laughing at something.

"Aednat was seduced long ago by Chaos. Long

before Balor ever came to her with a plan to release the demon. Chaos will always seek out those who are afraid, those who seek to control the world around them. Aednat was one of those. I begged her not to listen. The whispers of Chaos can always be found within the realms of the in-between, and she found Aednat."

The foggy image shifted and the two girls broke apart. Aednat lashed out at Fianna and then disappeared. Waving her hand over the picture, the queen wiped it away in a swirl of mist.

"I couldn't save her, Quinn. Chaos poisoned Aednat's mind, and I couldn't stop it, no matter how I loved her." Her voice dropped low, a tear slipped from her eye. "If I could have changed things, I would have, but Aednat . . ."

The screech of an owl broke through Fianna's remembrances. We both turned toward the huge bird that sat across from us on a large deadfall, it's huge eyes locked on the gateway that Bres had gone through.

"Bres does not have much more time," Fianna said.

I shivered, my skin rising in goose bumps all over my arms. "What happens if I go in now?"

"I do not know," she said, her face not giving

me even a flicker of emotion. "I doubt anything good."

Fantastic.

I rubbed my arms. "I can't wait any longer, I'm going after him."

She bowed her head, her shoulders slumping. "I will not stop you. I believe you are the Chosen One, and as such, you must be free to do as you see fit."

What did I say to that? I didn't want to tell her I didn't care, didn't want to say that the world could go to hell. Ashling was gone, Luke was dying, and I would lose Bres if I didn't act now. The only one who would maybe miss me if I didn't make it back was Lir.

"Tell my father I tried," I said, "If I don't make it back."

Leaping off the high ground, I sloshed my way toward the two gateways. The one filled with light almost vibrated with energy. It drew me like a child to a shiny object. I found my hands reaching toward that gateway before I could stop myself.

Clenching my fingers, I pulled back and faced the dark gateway. There was nothing particularly evil about it, more an absence of light than anything else.

"One last piece of advice, Quinn."

I turned to look back at Fianna.

"Do not lie. Be honest not only with those you meet, but with yourself and your own heart. Show the truth the respect it deserves."

As if it heard her words, my heart thumped painfully in my chest. I thought of Bres in there, fighting for me, fighting for Luke. He and Luke did not like each other, barely tolerated one another when they were working together, with reason it seemed. And yet for me, he would save his rival. Two quick strides, and I was standing directly in front of the darkened archway. The green leaves of the arbutus tree were incredibly vibrant against the black trunk. With one finger, I traced the leaf closet to me, the foliage shuddering under my fingertip.

A rush of air poured out of the gateway, the smell of the ocean heavy within it. Clenching my hands at my sides, I stepped through the arch, and found myself plunged into a raging ocean, the black of night surrounding me.

5

The dead of night, the darkness of a raging ocean and my fear for Bres roared over me as I stepped fully through the gateway.

Water rolled over me in crashing waves, shoving me in all directions. I didn't fight the waves or the current, just let them pull me where they wanted, and within minutes, I was thrown by a huge swell onto a rock-strewn beach, my body hitting the sandy ground hard enough to knock the wind out of me. For a brief second, I struggled to get my wind back, and with a gasp, finally drew air.

Blinking, I took me a moment to see the dark

shapes surrounding me and truly understand what I was seeing.

The helicopter pilot who'd died trying to fly us off the island.

The banshees I'd killed.

The Fomorii I'd killed.

And Aednat, her eyes narrowing as she stared at me. Slowly, I stood. None of them moved toward me and I didn't really know what to do.

"Why are you all here?" I asked, fearing I might already know the answer.

Aednat laughed. "You killed us, so now you must face your deeds, dark Fae. You must face the death you did cause."

My jaw clenched and I gave a nod. Truth. I had to be truthful. I took a breath and slowly spoke. "As much as I wish it weren't true, I'd do it all again, if I had to if it meant that I could save my sister, or Luke, or this world of ours."

The rat-faced banshee, who'd poisoned me and killed Cora, stepped forward. "Truly?"

"Yes."

Each of them stepped forward, one at a time, and I had to face them. The wounds I'd inflicted were still on their bodies, the blood still dripped. The Fomorii were the most numerous, thirteen in all. I didn't realize I'd ended so many lives when I'd fought them.

Aednat tipped her chin up and looked down her nose at me. "You killed us all. Now feel the pain of our deaths as if they were your own."

From the first Fomorii I'd killed, right on through to the banshees and Aednat, my body was suddenly pulled in every direction. The shock of my limbs being sliced into, my body ripped out of the helicopter, lit on fire, gutted, and slammed into with bolts of power, hit me all at once. Then the emotions hit. Fear of dying, the shame of losing to a Tuatha, anger and sorrow for those left behind, and even remorse. *Those* were worse than the physical pain. Sobbing, I held my head in my hands, the emotions more than I could deal with, so I just let them pour out of me in the tears that streamed down my face.

Combined, the pain in my body and in my heart left me feeling as if I were being pulled apart an inch at a time. I didn't fight any of it. I'd done this to them, the least I could do was honor it, respect it.

As suddenly as the pain and emotions had started, they stopped. Laid flat out, the sand was gritty against my tear-soaked cheek. With great care, I pushed myself to my feet, wobbling as I stood.

The ones I'd killed, directly or indirectly, still held a loose circle around me.

The helicopter pilot stepped forward first. "I am satisfied." A breeze blew in from the ocean and his image was dispersed as if it were made of smoke. One by one they stepped forward, stating the same thing until they'd all gone. Except for one.

Aednat.

"Aednat is not satisfied with your pain and suffering." She snapped.

A sharp crack of thunder and the bite of electricity sung through the air.

I spread my hands. "What would you have me do, Aednat? You threatened the life of my sister, you wanted to be Chaos's host body, you fought your sister who is a good queen. She is a good queen to the banshees to those you were supposed to protect."

She snapped her teeth at me. "You ruined Aednat's world she had made. You should die."

It was so simple for her as if she truly was a child. I scrubbed my hands over my face. "One day, I will die, probably very soon as I'm going to face

Chaos with no training. Is that not enough for you?"

She tipped her head and chewed her lower lip. "Perhaps. Aednat wishes to be there when the fatal blow is struck on you, that she may see your death with her own eyes."

"If it is possible to do that, then fine by me." What did I care who watched me die? If it made it so that I could move toward Bres and the cauldron, then so be it.

Aednat smile. "I am satisfied."

Her image dispersed on the wind and I was left alone on the beach.

With a stumble, I struck out down the beach. "How the hell am I going to know which way to the cauldron?" I asked the sand and waves.

To my amazement, they responded. The ground shifted, small pebbles began to form arrows, pointing back the way I'd come. Well, that seemed simple enough to follow.

Picking up speed, I began to run down the beach, the sand giving way with every other step, forcing me to slow my pace. "Bres, where are you?" I muttered. This time the pebbles didn't change.

It occurred to me then that Cora been silent for some time.

"Cora, any ideas?"

A stirring within me, as if she were waking up, rippled across my mind. *I am here. Follow the arrows. That is what I would do.*

I wiped at my face and looked up. A familiar figure was striding down the beach.

"Bres!" I shouted, jumping and running toward him. His eyes barely had time to register shock before he caught me in his arms and held me tight. I clung to him, relief flowing out of me. I'd found him.

"Quinn, what are you doing here?" he whispered into my hair. For just a moment, I let myself feel him against me, our hearts beating against each other, the scent of him filling me and soothing some of the fear. Shaking my head, I pushed out of his arms. "You were taking too long. Did you get the cauldron?"

He closed his eyes and shook his head. "I'm sorry. The cauldron refused to come with me. Quinn, you shouldn't have come here. I don't know how to get you out."

Remembering what Fianna had said about the cauldron having a life of its own, I nodded. "Do you think we could convince it? Together?"

"I don't know. Quinn, you have to know I didn't

charm you. I couldn't charm a mouse into eating cheese." He reached out and took my hand, his fingers curling around mine.

"I know. I'm sorry, but I had no reason believe Luke was lying," I said. Which begged the question, why *had* Luke lied? Not now, the time was not now for those questions.

Bres led me down the beach, following the pebbles that continued to show us the way. "Ah, maybe I would have done the same thing if I thought I could keep you all to myself." He gave me a lazy wink. I blushed, feeling the heat start in my belly and swirl outward. He was giving Luke an out, one that he didn't have to provide.

"Did you have to face . . ." I couldn't quite finish it. Bres gave me a sad smile. "Yes, though to be honest, I feel better now, knowing they are all satisfied with my answers."

"A lot of people?" I asked.

"Yes. Far too many. I wish there were less, but I've lived a life of fighting and blood for a very long time."

The pebbles led us around a huge piece of driftwood that stood well over my head, to the edge of a fire pit dug down into the sand, where a large bubbling pot hung over the open flames. The swirls of mist that spilled out of the pot were soft pink, the color of a newborn's skin, and the scent was one of apple pies and fresh spring air. I breathed in deeply, and let the smells permeate my lungs before I spoke.

"How do you talk to a cauldron?" I asked softly.

"You don't. You talk to its speaker," a voice from the far side of the fire said, then spat to the side.

Licking my lips, I sidestepped and peered around the large cauldron. A face peered back at me through the mist, an older gentleman in blue overalls. The speaker looked suspiciously like . . .

"Don?" I asked.

Bres leaned close. "Who's Don?"

"He gave us a ride in his pickup truck to Cameron Lake," I said, not sure if what I was seeing was real or some strange twist of my own mind.

Don grunted. "Well, you can't be the speaker all the time nowadays. Most people just think that the cauldron is a legend and don't even bother to look for it. So I got myself a real job. But just because we met before doesn't mean you can just take the cauldron." He lifted a finger at me, and then glared at Bres.

I crouched in front of him. "Please, do you

remember what you said to me, right before I got out of your truck?"

His eyes softened. "Refresh my memory."

"You told me love is precious and I shouldn't let it slip past me 'cause I was looking for something perfect," I whispered. "That's why we're here. Luke is dying, and . . ." I glanced up at Bres, then back at Don. "I need him. I need Luke to stand with me in these last battles. Just like I need Bres. Without them both, I won't be able to face what is coming. I know that now. I can't do this on my own, no matter what the prophecy says." The words settled over me, filling me with the truth of them. I needed both without any doubt.

Don smiled, his grin splitting his face. "Now, that's my girl. You let love rule your heart, and that is what will save us all."

Reaching out, he took my hand and pulled it toward the cauldron. "Stick your hand in there. You'll be marked, a brand as it were. Through the mark you will be able to heal Luke even if he's crossed over. But only if it's recent." Again, he lifted his finger to me. "If he's been dead more than an hour, you can't save him. Understand?"

Gritting my teeth, I plunged my hand into the cauldron, expecting the heat to be intense, the pain to be all-consuming, but the mist just engulfed my hand, and warmth spread up my arm as the pink fog clung to me. I swirled my hand about and, though I couldn't see it, dipping my hand deeply into the fluid within the cauldron.

"How long will it take?" I lifted my eyes to Don's.

"It's done," he said, motioning for me to take my hand out.

Standing, I pulled my hand out. There on the palm was etched a cup like the world's most intricate and detailed tattoo. Jewels stood out along the stem, and the base pearls and diamonds reflected the light around us back to me.

"You can use that mark to heal one time. One time only. If you use the cauldron a second time, you will likely lose your life."

"Likely?" I asked.

"Well, let's just say that it will take everything you have and then keep on taking." Don shook his head, a tear slipping from his eye. "So, just don't try a second time." Leaning over, he patted my cheek, his lips trembling. As he pulled away I saw the faint imprint of a cup—the same cup I now had on my hand—on his. A flash of insight hit me hard.

"That's how you lost your Mary, isn't it?" I whispered. "She used it twice."

Don nodded, the tears running freely now. "She was a brave girl, a beauty like you, but her heart was too big. I tried to get to her, but it was too late for her. She was gone too long." He sniffled and rubbed one big hand across his eyes. "Go on now, you don't need to have the same thing happen to you and your man. Go."

On impulse, I gave Don a hug, holding him tightly for a brief moment before leaping to my feet. I waved back to him as Bres and I ran down the beach. There was one final burning question I had.

"How do we get back to Fianna and the swamp?"

"We don't. You do," Bres said.

As if his words were the signal, something pulled on me, like a marionette string attached to my body that I'd been unaware of all along.

"No! I'm not leaving without you," I screamed. Before I could get yanked any farther, I leapt toward him, wrapping my arms around his waist. "Hang on to me. I'm not going to leave you behind."

His arms wound about me, but with every beat of his heart under my ear, I felt him fading.

No! Bres, fight for me! I screamed into his mind.

I'm trying, Quinn, he whispered back.

I struggled to hang onto him, tried to find a way to bury my hands into him so that whatever was trying to spit me back out into the swamp would take him too.

Love. Don had said love would save us. Maybe now would be a good time to not only listen to those words, but believe in them too. To put love into action.

Lifting my head, I pressed my lips to his, the kiss deepening without any effort. Bres's hands tangled into my hair and I forgot for just a moment why I'd kissed him and only knew that it was everything I wanted. The kiss was a fire that raced through my body, weakened my knees and drew a moan from my lips. His body seemed to solidify in more ways than one, his arms pinning me to his chest. My feet were lifted from the ground as we clung to each other, lips sealed. I wouldn't lose him, not again.

I needed him. He groaned against my mouth, his lips forming words that I wasn't following.

Someone cleared their throat. "Well, I see you

found him," Fianna said, though she seemed, to me, to be quite far away.

I could barely open my eyes, the languor of Bres's kiss stealing any ability I had to move fast. His hands were tight around me, one at my back and one right under my ass. "What happened?" I asked.

Bres smiled down at me, his eyes full of a hunger that we'd re-lit with one kiss. Good gravy, what would happen if Luke saw us like this? Did I care?

The cold from the swamp seeped back into me, but my left hand, the one with the cauldron's mark, was still pleasantly warm. Thoughts of Luke snapped me out of the moment.

"We have to hurry," I said, stepping back from Bres and untangling my arms from him, knowing I couldn't untangle my heart so easily, but then, I didn't really want to untangle my heart from him or Luke.

"Come, I will lead the way back," Fianna said. I finally looked over at her and frowned. The light around us was not anywhere near where it had been when I'd gone through the gateway. It was morning now, daybreak, and I'd gone through as the moon rose.

"How long were we in there?" I asked, hurrying to catch up with the queen.

"Almost all night. But I felt I should stay until dawn, in the hopes that you would be the one person to break the rules of the cauldron. I'm glad I waited. You would have been lost in the swamp without me," she said, her skirts swirling through the water around her.

Bres caught up to me and snagged my fingers. I gave them a squeeze. "Bres, I don't know what to do. I need you both." It was as much a gut feeling as the strings they'd each tied to my heart that made me feel that way. They were important to me on so many levels.

"I'll stand by you, no matter what, Quinn. Even if you choose Luke, I'll stand by you," he said, his voice soft, just for me.

Unable to speak, I nodded, squeezed his hand and reluctantly let go. I didn't deserve these two men in my life. Maybe Fianna was right, maybe having two men love you was a curse rather than a blessing.

We moved as fast as we could, emerging from the swamp along the northern edge of Cameron Lake. For a moment I paused, and stared out at the open water. There was no sign of Morty, the multitentacled, bad-attitude-filled monster that had nearly eaten me not once, but twice. Nor was there any sign of my father, Lir. He'd gone to rouse the old gods that were left, because he was certain there was going to be a battle with Chaos. Everyone was certain that a battle was coming.

I had my doubts though about said battle. I didn't think that Chaos was going to let me get close enough to raise a weapon against her. Not knowing that she believed the prophecy, not knowing that she believed that I would kill her. Why would she let me get close enough to fight her?

"Quinn?" Fianna's voice drew me back to the present. "We have to hurry."

She stepped up our pace and we had to jog to keep up with her as she floated along the lake's edge.

"How much farther?" I asked, hopping over the crushed hull of a small rowboat as we rounded a point on the shoreline.

Fianna didn't answer, only picked up her speed again.

A ripple in the water and a soft splash caught my attention. Rising out of the lake, directly in front of us was Lir, his body covered in a dark blue robe.

"Lir! Over here!" I yelled, waving my arm. I could only hope he had good news, that he'd been able to wake the other gods. That we would have people that stood with us against Chaos.

He ran toward us across the water. My breath caught in my throat. Something was wrong. What could have happened? I couldn't pinpoint it, but my instincts whispered that I was once more in trouble.

"Quinn, get out of the way!" Bres shouted, shoving me to one side as Lir's blade came hurtling through the air at me. A flash of silver and the brush of the air it disturbed was all I felt before I hit the ground, the soggy bank absorbing my fall.

Bres stepped in front of me, his sword raised as Lir engaged him. "So, you've switched sides again, eh, Bres?"

That wasn't Lir's voice.

It was Card's.

6

I'd mistaken Card for Lir, they were of similar build and with the blue robe on covering his head I'd thought it was my father. A flash of his golden eyes confirmed that I was looking at my half-brother as he raised his weapon to Bres.

The two men squared off, swords slamming into one another with a speed I couldn't follow except for the blur of metal. Fianna was on the far side of them, her eyes wide and concerned even at that distance.

"Quinn, go. Save Luke, I got this wee prick," Bres said through gritted teeth.

They swept their weapons back and forth so quick that I could barely see the shimmer of the metal.

Card pulled a dagger with his free hand and raised it to throw at me. I dove to the side, but that move of his drew Bres out of form and left him open. "Quinn, get out of here!"

I saw it in my mind a split second before it happened so it was like seeing a double image.

Card winked at me then, with a twist of his right hand, unarmed Bres, and slammed the butt of his sword into Bres's temple.

Bres slid to the ground, body limp and unconscious. Card held up his sword, poised to drive it down through Bres's back. "Yes, sister, go save little Lugh while I finish off Bres."

"Cora," I whispered.

You don't have a choice, Quinn. You can't outrun this battle. You must face your brother now.

I nodded and pulled my dagger out, gripping it with my right hand. Bres was an amazing swordsman. If he couldn't beat Card, I didn't have a hope in hell. But he'd been distracted

"That? You're going to face me with that puny little dagger?" Card snorted. "All right then, sister, if you insist. Are you ready to die?"

"Not today, Card," I said with false bravado. "Only one of us is dying, and it isn't going to be me."

He circled me and I followed him, not letting him get behind me. Card moved like the sharks he could command, smooth and easy with a predatory grace that completely unnerved me.

I stepped back and he followed, his blue eyes glinting. He lunged at me, his sword swiping toward my middle. I leapt backward, just deflecting the tip of the sword, keeping it from tearing into my stomach—but barely. It stripped through my t-shirt, slicing it open.

Again and again, Card came at me, the speed and power behind his attacks pushing me deeper into the swamp, back the way we'd come. It took everything I had to keep his blade from cutting into me, and I could tell he wasn't even trying. He was playing with me. This tactic of mine was not working. I had to outsmart him. I couldn't outfight him.

I lifted my left hand ever so slightly, preparing to use a bolt of power.

"I wouldn't do that if I were you, little sister. You don't want to challenge me for control over my natural element," he said as calmly as if we were discussing a Sunday crossword over tea. The bastard wasn't even out of breath. I was puffing hard and using everything I had to keep him off me and that was with all the strength and speed that quickening had done for me.

"Oh, don't worry. I wasn't going to do anything with the water," I said, and unleashed the bolt. He dived to the left, but the bolt caught him in one shoulder and spun him around. He disappeared beneath the shallow murky surface.

Before he could get up, I leapt toward him, flinging my dagger, propelling it with a second power bolt. I had no idea if it nailed him or not. I couldn't see through the dirt we'd stirred up. Calling my dagger back to my hand, I stood there at the edge of the swamp, panting for air as much as from exertion as from adrenaline.

The water around me stilled and I held my breath. His body didn't float to the surface, mortally wounded or otherwise. I scanned the area, desperately searching for a sign that I'd finished him off. No, it wasn't to be that easy.

Hands gripped my ankles, and yanked me down into the water. I kicked out, catching Card in the head. He let go and we both scrambled to our feet, water dripping off us. I swiped at my face, clearing the drips from my vision.

"You little bitch! I'm going to steal your power." He rolled his shoulders, cracked his knuckles.

"And then I'm going to kill you and feed you to Morty."

Card slid his sword back into its scabbard and came at me with his bare hands. It shouldn't have been more terrifying than having him coming at me with a weapon, but it was. That he wanted to strangle me was a far more intimate death than I was comfortable with.

Stumbling backward, I fought to stay away from him while his laughter chased me. Fianna stood silent on the edge of the swamp. I slammed into a barrier, bouncing off it and hitting the ground hard. It took me about half a second to realize that Card had trapped me with him inside a barrier, effectively blocking any attempt either Fianna or Bres might make to help me.

Son of a bitch!

Fingers tangled in my hair and Card yanked me tightly against him, my back flush against his chest. "Don't worry," he whispered into my ear. "I'll kill you quickly. You see, I can be merciful. Our father would want that."

One of his hands gripped my jaw and the other rested lightly on my left breast, over my heart. A pulse of energy swirled around us.

His fingers dug into me, biting at my flesh as

my powers slowly began to slip away from me. This was what Luke had warned me about. I struggled, but it was no use, not against both Card's physical strength and his innate powers. He was stronger than me on both fronts.

Fight him, Quinn! You can turn the tables on him! Bres's voice inside my head steadied me. He stood at the edge of the barrier, his eyes pleading with me. There was nothing he could do on that side of the barrier that Card had made. I was on my own.

Bres is right, if you take Card's power, you may be strong enough to break Chaos's hold on Ashling, Cora said.

A swell of sudden hope that maybe I *could* save Ashling after all was what I needed to fight back. With a cry, I flung myself backward into Card, throwing us both to the ground. Yanking hard, I freed myself from his hand on my jaw and turned to face him, slamming my hand over his heart.

"Card, stand with me against Chaos," I said, hoping he would see it was the smart thing to do.

"Or?"

"We end this now."

With a roar, he tried to buck me off. Feeling the connection he'd established between us, I drew on it, stealing his power the same way he'd taken mine. He tried to block me, the power stuttering. I thought of Ashling trapped by Chaos. Everything depended on me doing this. I wouldn't fail my little sister again. I wouldn't fail her, or Luke, or Bres.

As fast as I could, I pulled Card's power into me, blowing through his every effort to stop me. But he was so strong that even as I took his power, he fought me. We rolled across the ground, Card pummeling me with his fists. I didn't lift my hands to protect myself. If I didn't take his power now, it wouldn't matter. I wouldn't be able to save myself or Ashling.

My lip and cheek were split, one eyelid swelled shut, but I wouldn't release my hand over his heart. He twisted my arm and I screamed as it cracked, but my fingers never left his skin.

He sat on top of me, my right hand curled into the flesh of his chest, blood oozing out from under my fingertips. The connection between us didn't flicker, not once.

I was not going to lose to him.

He took a deep gasping breath. "Ah, I should have known you'd be the death of me. Chosen One. A whore's child. Not worthy." He began to sag under my hand.

Pausing in the taking of his power, I asked him again. "Stand with me, Card. Please. Don't make me do this."

"Never. You should never have been born. I was to be his heir." He spat the words at me, his eyes sunk into his head, full of hatred and fury even as his body shriveled. "There can be only one of us."

Tears pricked my eyes. "Then this is it. Good-bye, brother."

He grimaced, took one last swing at me, his fist bouncing feebly off my forehead. I closed my eyes, prayed that this would be the last death on my hands, and took the last drops of his power, and, with it his life.

7

C ard's power flushed through me, but it was a bittersweet strength. I'd killed my brother to survive, killed him with the hope that maybe I could be strong enough to save Ashling. Maybe.

Bres lifted Card off me, rolling his body to one side before he gathered me up into his arms. Sobs rippled out of me, uncontrollable. I didn't remember starting to cry, didn't remember the barrier coming down.

I could see Card's eyes, the hatred in them still and yet I hadn't wanted to hurt him. I hadn't wanted to be backed into that corner.

"Quinn, you be all right." Bres's hands rubbed

my back. "Come on, we have to go. Luke, we have to get you to Luke."

He was right, there was no time to feel this sorrow. We had to move fast. Wobbling to my feet, a rush of awareness I'd never had filled my senses. Every drop of water was mine to command, from the lake, to the rain, to the moisture beading on Bres's forehead.

I took a slow even breath, gingerly holding my broken arm against my chest. "Let's go."

Pausing, I stared down at Card's shrunken body, half covered in the water. "Fianna will you. . ." was all I managed before she interrupted me.

"We will take care of his body." She inclined her head to me.

Bres took off his shirt and twisted it into a bandage to bound up my broken arm. It hurt, but already I could feel the break knitting, the split in my lip and my swollen eye healing.

Bandaged and on my feet, moments later Bres and I were running as fast as we could. Moments later we burst into the banshee's bower, startling the guards on duty.

"Where's Luke?" I asked.

She pointed to the back of the bower, and the trees leaned outward to reveal the way. With Bres at my heels, I bolted down the path, skidding to a halt in a second clearing. Luke lay on a bed of flowers, his hands folded over his far too still chest.

"No," I whispered. We were too late.

Bres grabbed my good arm. "The old man said there was a time that you could call Luke back from death."

The banshee guard followed us into the clearing, Fianna close behind. "How long has he been dead?"

The guard shrugged. "A while, I suppose."

Fianna stepped up. "With the time that has already passed where he can be brought back, you will have wasted the healing power of the cauldron if you use it now."

"I'll take that chance," I said.

Dropping to my knees beside Luke's body, I reached out, then paused, staring at Card's blood still cooling on my fingers. I closed my eyes to block out the sight.

Damn, I knew there was something I'd forgotten. "How do I make the cauldron work?" I asked.

Fianna came to my side and pressed my hand over Luke's silent heart. "Here. It is like all magic; you must *will* the healing to begin."

Pressing my palm hard into his cold skin, I

prayed we weren't too late. The warmth in my arm slid down to my fingers, the skin on Luke's chest around my hand slowly gained color. "Come on, Luke, this isn't the end, not yet. I still have to kick your ass for lying to me," I whispered.

Bres crouched beside me. "He's a fighter. We aren't too late. He won't dare give you up to me without at least one argument of why he is better than me."

But nothing happened, despite the warmth in my hand and the color on his chest changing. Luke didn't take a breath. He didn't pink up other than around my hand.

"Come on, please don't die on me. I'll let the whole lie about Bres slide, if you just come back. We need you, Luke. Your time here isn't done." There was nothing, not even a glimmer of movement. This wasn't fair! We'd fought so hard! I wanted to hit something, to lash out. Anything to not feel this gaping hole. I couldn't lose him. I couldn't lose another person I cared about.

Slipping my broken arm out of the sling, I put my other hand on his forehead. "Damn it, Luke!" I yelled, "Don't you dare back out on me now!"

A bright flare of heat snapped between my hand and his chest, jerking his body like an electric shock. The intensity of the light dulled my eyes. I turned my head, but didn't let go of him.

"Ashling? Don't leave." Luke groaned out the words. Luke.

My head whipped around so hard, I smacked into Bres, giving me temporary stars. "Luke?" I was afraid my eyes were deceiving me. He had rumpled hair, bags under his eyes and a gaunt frame from the poison burning through his system, but he was alive.

Luke started to sit up, but I pushed him back down. "No, you can't. Not yet. You've been . . .dead."

"Dead? I feel fine, are you sure I was . . ." He paused. "I thought for a minute there that you were your sister. I saw her when I was dreaming. What happened? Where's Aednat?" he asked. Then his eyes flicked to Bres. "What the hell?" Rolling away from me, Luke got to his feet and shot a ball of fire at Bres, who ducked the flames and spun out of the way.

"Luke, stop!" I yelped, ducking under a second gout of flame. "He's on our side! It was Chaos who showed him the vision about me killing Ashling! He's not with Balor!"

Bres continued to dodge the fire, though I could see it was wearing on him. I did the only thing I could. Running to Bres, I pressed my back against his chest and faced Luke. "Stop this. I need you both to stand with me. Please, Luke. Bres helped me save your life. He was ready to give up his own to save yours which is not something you just randomly do."

Luke looked down at me, his eyes full of confusion. "What happened?"

I quickly explained about Aednat, the poison, and the cauldron. When I got to the part about Card, the pain of it hit me in the gut like a punch. I sank to my knees. I'd killed my brother, and though I didn't love him like I loved Ashling, what did it say of me that I could do it at all? That I could take a siblings life?

Luke's arms gingerly went around me, and I let my body collapse against his. I was exhausted and heart sore, and we still had so very, very far to go. Excalibur, the three Smiths, and Chaos all loomed ahead of me, of us.

A second set of hands touched my back and I reached for Bres. Luke stiffened. "I need you both," I said. He relaxed and Bres gripped my one hand, his fingers interlocking with mine.

"We have to keep her safe," Bres said, as if I weren't even there.

"Agreed," Luke answered. "When this is done we'll figure everything else out then."

I grunted and closed my eyes, feeling grateful for this one moment of respite. It was far from perfect, but I suspected it was all I was going to get.

Fianna came to stand beside us. "You should rest before you seek out the three Smiths. Luke, while you may be feeling up to the task, your body should still heal. Bres and Quinn, you should rest too after your fight for the cauldron and what came after." She never mentioned Card by name, for which I was glad.

Two banshees led us to a third bower. This one was smaller and felt cozy. Three beds were made up of cedar bows, moss and maple leaves. They looked heavenly to me. How long had it been since I'd slept properly? I couldn't even remember. I'd been running on fairy honey and adrenaline for too long to recall.

I crashed on the middle one, my eyes shutting as the two men spoke softly in the background. I didn't care, as long as they didn't start fighting, they could talk all night. But I found myself staying awake to hear them.

"Why did you tell her I charmed her?" Bres

asked. "You know I have no ability with that, you had to know she'd find out eventually."

Luke grunted. "Because I could see how hung up she was on you turning against her. You about broke her heart when you said you didn't trust her. I thought it was better that way, for her to believe it was a clean break. How was I to know it was Chaos showing you visions, making you distrust Quinn? I didn't think you'd be coming back."

"Next time, perhaps you should consider telling the truth. Women always find a man's lies, no matter how well he thinks he's hidden them." Bres laid down on the bed to my left by the creak of it.

Luke grunted again, and with that they went quiet, apparently satisfied.

I relaxed and sleep claimed me immediately— but then, so did the dream. I was still in the bower but both boys were sleeping. They had moved their beds close to mine, one on either side.

How was it that I could love them both? Was that even allowed? I brushed the hair back off Luke's forehead, feeling the silken texture of it run across my fingers. Turning to Bres, I did the same, my heart beating hard for both of them.

"Well, that's a problem I'd like to have."

I stood, my eyes seeing her, but my mind not believing who was in front of me.

Ashling stood across from me, her petite frame wrapped in an off-the-shoulder white gown that was fitted over her hips, flaring into a wide skirt that trailed out around her like a wedding gown's train. I looked down at my grubby jeans and T-shirt, cut and torn and covered in blood that was not my own, surprised that the garments were even still intact.

She stepped toward me and I held up my hand. "How do I know it's you and not Chaos?" Gods, the pain in her eyes nearly buckled my knees.

Ashling started to cry. "Please, I only have a short time. While she sleeps, my spirit can wander. It's the only moment I have."

That was all I could take. There was still a chance it was a trap, but I would run that risk. Three strides and I pulled her into my arms, her sobs muffled into my shoulder. "Quinn, I'm so scared. I'm not strong enough to fight her. She's crushing me. I'm losing myself."

I held her tightly, not knowing what to say. "I'm still fighting for you. You can't give up."

"You have to kill my body. It's the only way to

stop her." She spoke against me her words muffled. I wasn't letting her go until I had to.

"Hush, don't talk like that. It isn't the only way. Cora said I could free you if I took Card's power," I said, smoothing her hair down her back. The curls tangled in my fingers. In such a short time, we'd come so far. My hands still had spots of Card's blood, there was swamp mud under my fingernails and the faintest etching of the cauldron remained on the palm of my hand. Against her strawberry blonde hair, my hands looked as if they belonged to a criminal.

"I think Cora lied to you," Ashling said, pulling back so she could look up at me. Her green eyes spilled over with tears. "I want to believe that you can save me, Quinn. I want to. But . . ."

I shushed her. "No, we won't end up apart. I promise you that. I won't give up."

"Say hi to Luke for me," she said, her eyes brightening. "I stayed with him while he floated in between life and death. He's cute, and sweet," Then she nodded, and flinched. "I have to go. She's waking up. I'll try to come again. And, Quinn... thank you for stopping Card. Chaos has been rewarding him by . . ." she swept her hand up and down her own body. "Even though it's not really mine anymore . . ." her voice broke and she stepped back. She lifted her hand and disappeared.

Anger like I'd never felt before ripped through me. Card had been using Ashling's body for a play toy. As a reward from Chaos.

"SON OF A BITCH!" I yelled, wishing I could kill him all over again. Any regrets I'd had were washed away in that moment of rage. It was enough to make me believe I was one of the dark Fae the amount of murderous wrath that coursed through me. There was nothing righteous about this anger, only bright pulsing fury that left me shaking and sick to my stomach.

Still in the dream I paced the bower until I began to calm. He couldn't touch her anymore. That was the only upside I could see to this moment, I'd killed him and ended what he had been doing to her.

Moving slowly, I went back to my bed and laid down on the moss filled bed. Staring straight up at trees that covered us, I couldn't see the night sky or the stars. Tears trickled out the corners of my eyes and down the sides of my face. Bres shifted on my one side and pulled me into his arms, cradling my body against his. He said nothing, only held me against the warmth of him. Reaching out, I touched Luke's hip and urged him closer, tucking his back against my belly. I tucked one arm up under Luke's head, and reached back with the other hand to pull Bres tightly against me.

Held between the two men, I fell back asleep, my tears drying, fading into determination with the knowledge that Ashling was still waiting for me to save her, that for the moment, she was still inside her body.

And if there was one thing I'd learned, it was that while love might not always conquer, it never gave up.

"I won't give up, Ash," I whispered. "I won't give up."

8

The dreams of the night faded and my sleep was undisturbed for what remained of the darkest hours.

Morning dawned cool with a light mist dusting down over our bodies, and I was even happier to be pressed between my two fae men, their body heat fending off the chill of the air. Not to mention it was a damn nice sight to wake up to the two impossibly handsome guys.

"Morning," Bres rumbled in my ear, his lips taking advantage of their proximity to my sensitive lobes, nibbling along the edges. Luke cradled my hand over his heart, but there was no heat there, not like what I was receiving from Bres. Still, it was very nice to be stuck between them, and I wasn't going to complain or move.

"Mmm." This was too good to be real. I had to still be dreaming.

"I think we'd best get moving," Luke said, patting my hand like I was a good kid, and totally breaking the spell as he let go of me, and stretched out on the ground, his vertebrae popping and cracking. I let out a sigh and sat up, looking down on my grubby clothes. Scrubbing my hand over my face and into the tangle of knots that had once been my hair I let out another sigh. "What I wouldn't give for clean clothes and a shower."

Bres laughed. "What's the point? We just have to go deeper into the forest to find the three Smiths. They don't be looking for fancy clothes to be impressed by."

"You're a guy, you wouldn't understand," I grumped, stretching as I stood, feeling several vertebrae of my own pop. Despite sleeping on the ground and dreaming of Ashling, I was completely refreshed. Glancing over my shoulder at Luke and Bres, I had no doubt they were the reason.

They had their heads bowed together, dark and light nearly touching. Luke nodded. "That seems to be the best course of action."

I frowned. "What does?"

Both of them looked over at me, their eyes far too innocent for anything good. "We were trying to figure out who should go to Nuadha," Luke said.

Bres dusted his hands off onto his pants. "We were thinking that you and Luke should go to Nuadha, speak to him, and try to convince him that Chaos is here and is a true threat. Then he can raise an army to stand at your back."

Lifting an eyebrow, I said, "And Bres, what about you?"

"Then Bres will go deeper into the forest and try to find a gateway to the three Smiths. I don't believe even Fianna knows which one it is," Luke said.

"Let me think a minute," I said, turning my back on them. *Cora, please, please still be here.*

I am here. Her voice was the calm I needed.

Lir didn't trust Nuadha. He even made Balor promise to keep me away from him, I said. *I can't go with Luke, can I?*

She was quiet a moment before she answered.

Nuadha may see you as a threat to his power. You are, after all, supposed to take his place. Go with your instincts, Quinn. They won't lead you astray. You have done well so far, better than even I had hoped.

There was one other thing I needed to ask Cora, no matter how awkward it was. Ashling thought Cora had led me wrong and I had to ask.

Did you lie to me? About Card's powers and freeing Ashling?

She retreated deep within me and no amount of prodding could make her come forward again. Her silence damned her and her lies. Scrunching my eyes shut, I took a few deep breaths to calm my hurt and the crushed hope that had started to bloom again.

I knew why Cora had said what she'd said. I wouldn't have fought Card as hard as I'd needed to if I didn't believe Ashling's life was on the line. She'd said what she'd said to make me strong enough, and I couldn't fault her that.

"Do you be all right, Quinn?" Bres asked.

I waved at him over my shoulder. "Give me a minute."

Cora had lied to me. I might not always fight hard for myself, but for Ashling I would give everything I had, and Cora knew that about me. Damn.

Without being able to speak with her, I had to go on what I did know. I agreed with Cora about following my instincts. The only problem now would be trying to get the boys to see the truth of it.

Turning back to them, they tensed the minute I met their eyes. "You're right, Luke, you need to convince Nuadha of the danger that is coming. That is important." They started to relax and I lifted my hand. "But I can't come with you. Nuadha . . .he will not welcome me. I will go with Bres to the three Smiths and get Excalibur remade."

Bres's eyebrows shot up, and a small smile played along the edge of his lips that Luke did not see.

Luke frowned. "Do you really think that's the best course?"

He was starting to trust me. I only hoped that I wasn't making the wrong decision. "Yes. I . . . I saw it when I was on the other side of the veil, when I was dying. And Lir confirmed it, Nuadha will not welcome me. Go to the camp, and then send word back to Fianna. We will find you from here. Hopefully, with a weapon that has the power to destroy Chaos."

Luke stepped forward and pulled me into his arms, hugging me tightly. "Be safe, Quinn. Please, please be safe." I tilted my head up for a kiss, but he brought his lips to my forehead in a gesture that was almost . . . brotherly. He looked away from me and cleared his throat. "Ashling would want you to be safe, above all else. Remember that."

Was he feeling awkward around Bres? That seemed the most likely cause. Luke stepped away, heading out the far side of the bower toward the lake. "You be safe too. I can't bring you back from the dead again." I tried to smile, but my lips were trembling too much. Something had changed between us, and it was more than just Bres being back. It was subtle, but there, nonetheless.

Watching him go, I wished I didn't have to see him walk away from me. It felt too much like a final goodbye. Too much like it wouldn't ever be the way it was before. Without knowing how, I knew this was a turning point, whether for good or for ill was all that was left to be decided.

"We should get moving." Bres touched my arm. We turned to see Fianna waiting behind us, her hands clasped in front of her.

"I have no help to give you on this next leg of your journey, Quinn. Only I bid you to take this." She handed me a brown drawstring bag about the size of a golf ball. "Do not open it now. You will know when the time is right."

Tucking the bag into my back pocket, I smiled.

"Thank you for all your help, and for your friendship."

She smiled back and my heart flipped. Her smile in that moment was so like Aednat's grin that it hurt me to see it.

I led the way out of the bower, the pain in my heart driving me with the memories of the little banshee I'd thought was my friend, that I thought was like a little sister to me. It seemed like I was destined to be the one to kill those I'd thought to protect, to end the lives of those around me. Bres caught up to me, matching his pace to mine.

"Do you know where we be headed?" he asked.

"No."

"Then . . .how exactly do you think we are going to be finding the Smiths?"

I paused in mid-stride and looked at him. "I don't know. I just figured we'd find them?"

Bres shook his head. "I don't think it be that easy. What about your pa? Could he help?" Now there was a thought. Of course, Lir was off on his own quest, hopefully having better luck than we were. The only way I knew how to contact him involved taking a nap, and I didn't think that would happen any time soon. While no one was in immediate danger, dillydallying wasn't going to be all that helpful.

Bres put his hands on his hips and dropped his chin to his chest. "You took Card's powers. Can you use them to seek out the Smiths?"

I opened my mouth to answer him that I didn't know, then snapped it shut. The birds had gone silent around us, even the air seemed to have stilled. Bres's head turned slowly, and he pulled his sword free of his scabbard with a slow slide of metal on metal.

Lifting his hand, he pointed for me to stay behind him. Trusting his judgement, I followed a few feet back, far enough that if he swung his sword, I wouldn't be in the way, but still close enough that I could help if needed.

He pointed at a thick bush, one heavy with foliage and trembling as if something or someone, hid within it.

Ever so slowly, he slid his sword into the bush, then stopped. "Come out. Before I slit your throat."

His sword followed our stalker's movement as the person slid out from behind the bus.

If you had given me a hundred guesses, I would not have given the name of the person who was on our trail.

Balor.

Bres dropped the tip of his sword and his jaw. "Pa." Then as if realizing just who it was, his sword snapped back up. "You'll not be getting past me to her. "

Balor shook his head, his arm clutching his middle. "I'm not here for that. I'm . . .dying. It took my last strength to bring me this far. I wanted to see you, Bres, one last time."

He held his hand out and a gush of blood flowed from his side through a wound I couldn't have spanned with both my hands. He gripped his body once more, barely staunching the flow. But Bres, surprising me, didn't go to him.

"Chaos, did this, didn't she?" I whispered, knowing it to be the truth. Balor nodded, and sunk to his knees.

"Yes, she stole Ashling from us. I was so wrong to fear you, Quinn, when it was me who brought Chaos on us all." His head drooped, yet I still didn't know if I could trust him, or if it was some sort of sham he was pulling on us.

"Bres, can you do anything to help him?" I asked. Bres shook his head, his jaw tight. But he slowly went to his father's side.

I crouched so we were eye to eye. "Balor, can

you help us find the three Smiths?" I asked. "That is all you can do now to help us stop her, to right the wrong you loosed on this world."

Again he nodded. "There is a rhyme of sorts that I remember from when I was a boy. You have to understand, it was a silly rhyme, one that meant nothing to me then, but perhaps now it might help you find your way to them." He took a slow breath that was wet with blood, and then spoke the rhyme.

"Over the hall,

Through the fall,

Cross the vale,

Between the shale,

There the Smiths of three prevail." He let out a cough, and the only thing I could think of was how bad a rhyme it was. But if it helped us find the Smiths then it didn't matter how bad or how corny it seemed to me.

"Thank you," I said.

"You will try to save her, won't you?" Tears streamed down his face as he lifted his eyes to mine, a father's tears for his only daughter.

"That's what I've been trying to do all along," I said, my voice gentle. "I will do everything I can to save her from Chaos."

A low groan escaped the man who'd so terrified me when we'd first met, and Bres finally dropped to his knees. He helped his father to lie down. "Pa, what happened?"

"Chaos attacked me and took control of the Fomorii. I couldn't kill her. Not even now." He turned his head to me. "I love her. She's my daughter. Tell her that when you save her. That all I did was because I didn't want her to come to harm."

I nodded, unable to speak past the catch in my throat. His next words chilled me. "And don't go to Nuadha, if you can help it. He's out for your blood, Quinn. He'll kill you if he gets even half a chance."

Lifting his hand to Bres's face, he whispered, "I was always proud of you, my boy, even when you rebelled. You are a better man than I could ever be. Don't let anyone change who you are."

I put a hand on Bres's shoulder as Balor's violet eyes closed, his breath hitched once, twice, and then his body went still. I wanted to give Bres time to say goodbye, time to make his peace. But there wasn't any left for us. No time, no peace, and no more chances.

"Bres." I sat beside him and hugged him, holding him as tightly as I could. "I'm sorry."

He said nothing, just held onto me. I leaned

back so I could see into his eyes. They were dry, not a single tear had fallen for his father. "I cannot cry for him, not after all he's done. He caused this, all of this. And now he dies when he could do the most good."

Pushing up, he pulled us both to our feet. "We need to go. If Chaos has control of the Fomorii, I've no doubt that she sent someone to watch where Balor went. Which means we are out of time."

And just like that, our fortunes shifted again.

He put his sword away and tugged me forward. We broke into a jog, keeping a steady pace together. As we rounded about a large tree, a banshee swept into view, her skirt swirling around a pair of cloven hooves instead of feet. She held up a hand. "Fianna sent me to tell you that the Fomorii have breached the forest outskirts. You must flee as do we!"

She spun as if to leave, Bres grabbed my hand, and I put on the brakes. "Wait!"

I waved at the banshee. "Over the hall, through the fall, cross the vale, between the shale, there the Smiths of three prevail. Does that mean anything to you?"

"The Hall of the Dead is the place where we

rest our souls. It's that way. That is the only hall of which I know." She pointed to the northeast.

That was all we needed, and all we were going to get. Sprinting, we followed her directions, fear driving us. While we were both strong, I wasn't fully trained, and the Fomorii were no longer ruled by someone who loved Bres.

The deep-throated howl of Fomorii's undead hounds spurred us on faster.

If we get to the three Smiths . . . I let the thought hang between Bres and me.

He answered, and it was what I was hoping. *If we get to them, ta Fomorii won't be able to pass their gates. There we will find safety for a time.*

It was all I needed. We burst through a thick patch of huckleberries and right into the Hall of the Dead. Calling it a hall did not give me the true understanding of what it actually was—a graveyard. The land had been stripped as if cleared by hand, and then what remained had been burned to the ground, the dirt beneath our feet was nothing but ash and bits of bone. Everything within the hall was black, and our feet left little puffs of smoke as we ran the length of the banshees' final resting place.

A screech behind us made me look over my

shoulder. Hounds of the undead skidded to a stop at the edge of the hall, sniffing the ground. Heads on bodies that didn't match, limbs protruding at weird angles, they snapped and snarled at each other. Even at that distance, I could see their teeth, razor sharp like all the Fomorii. In a sudden boiling mass, they pushed forward, only to have the forerunner sucked downward into the graves with barely a yelp. The others retreated, snarling and snapping their teeth but not so foolish as to try their luck.

"They're undead. They can't get through the hall," Bres said. "They'll have to go around."

Another glance showed me that, indeed, the hounds had figured out that going around was their way to us. It bought us a little time, not much, but more than we had a moment before.

Now, we only had to look for the fall. That is if what Balor had told us was right.

That is if we weren't on the wrong track.

9

Leaving behind the blasted ground of the hall of the dead, we had a short lead on the Fomorii undead hounds. Their howls though, grew ever closer despite them losing members to the banshees' graves when they strayed too far into the burnt and desolate land.

Unable to spare breath for talking, I questioned Bres mind to mind. *Fall, what the hell is a fall?*

It could be falls, like a waterfall, he answered.

We need to stop then, I can't hear anything over my heart beating, and how hard I'm breathing.

Skidding to a stop, I held my breath. In the distance, the rush of water falling over rocks reached my ears. Bres tipped his head and pointed above the trees. "There. See the mist curling over the tree tops? That be where we are headed."

I could see what he was pointing at in the far distance—the gauzy film above the cedars and fir was just discernible. It was all we needed. Bolting in that direction, we were again running at full speed, dodging trees and leaping over stumps as fast as we could. But our stop to find our direction had cost us. Thirty strides into our run, the hounds were on us, teeth snapping at our heels, lunging in their attempts to hamstring us.

I spun, and held my hands out, called my fire to my fingertips and unleashed it on the hounds, knowing it would roast them, but I hadn't counted on Card's power flowing through my veins.

There was a moment of pain that dropped me to my knees.

"Quinn!" Bres was at my side in an instant grabbing at me to pull me to my feet. Only I couldn't move.

Power like nothing else I'd felt roared upward through me, strangling me with the intensity of it. The hounds were coming faster and I knew that I had to do something quick. Biting back the pain of using the power I'd taken from Card, I lifted my hand and called the power that was at my fingertips upward and sent it out in a blast of fire.

Blue flames curled outward like a wave of water and quickly enveloped the pack in a mushroom cloud fire, bigger than anything I'd ever even thought I could do.

The undead dogs slammed into one another trying to avoid the flames, but the cloud enveloped them. Their howls lasted a split second before cutting off in mid cry.

Shaking, I lowered my hands. The power rushing through me made my skin crawl as if it were too much for my body. I didn't like it. It felt as though the power was in control and not me. The flames continued to lick along the charred bodies of the hounds, their flesh crisped black like the ash we'd only just come through.

"Quinn, are you all right?" Bres asked. A quick bob of my head was all I could manage.

He touched my arm. "That was well done, but we've got to go. There will be more than that behind us. They have our scent."

Again we ran, this time toward the growing sound of the waterfalls. At certain moments, I wasn't sure if what I was experiencing was real, the running drew me into an almost trance-like state.

My body was doing the work, keeping me moving, as I stayed close to Bres, but my mind wandered.

A week ago, I'd been your average twenty-two-year old. A week ago Ashling had been safe. Life had been good. I'd understood my place in the world. I'd been struggling but everything had been relatively within the realm of what you would call normal.

Now I was running through a forest from creatures I hadn't known existed. I couldn't stop wondering if I would wake up, if this was all some sort of bad dream that had sucked me into another world. But if that was the case, I'd not have met Bres.

I'd have not met Cora.

I'd have not found my strength that while it still wavered at times, was growing with each challenge I faced.

Beside me Bres breathed hard, leaping obstacles and helping me with a hand wherever he could, and I knew in those moments that I would take on all the monsters in the world to have Bres at my side. Maybe it wasn't love, maybe it was, but whatever was between us was strong and true and he hadn't lied or charmed to get me to see him for who he was.

We're almost there. His words interrupted my thoughts. I snapped back to the present and really looked at the place where we were.

Rocks littered our path and they were getting bigger as we hit the stream and made our way up to the head of the water where the waterfall spilled into a deep clear pool of vibrant blue water.

"Through the fall," I whispered. "We have to go in?"

"That's what I'd say." Bres nodded. "Together?"

I nodded and without another question, we dove into the pool in tandem, breaking through the surface and coming up together. Swimming toward where the waterfall spilled into the pool, I could see behind the curtain of it a hazy image of a door etched into a rock wall. Could it be that easy?

"Do you see it?" I yelled over the crashing of the waterfall.

"Yes!"

To be fair, after all we'd been through I half expected something to wrap around our ankles and pull us under, or to have some other obstacle thrown our way. The tension rose in me as we swam and I kept looking over my shoulder expecting to see another Fomorii, or some other monster.

We pulled ourselves over the rocks as the water from the falls pounded our bodies hard. Every rock was covered in slime, and it made gripping them damn near impossible. I slipped and smacked my face on a rock, Bres slipped and I heard a snarled curse.

The water slammed into my back and I finally closed my eyes and made my way by feel.

Bres made it out first, then reached back to help me stand behind the waterfall.

From behind the raging waters, we watched an army of Fomorii range on the banks of the river. An army of them. All to take on Bres and me.

That was the tension I'd been feeling.

"Shit," I said. Bres tugged on my arm and we scuttled toward the door. There was a single image etched into the door, though door would make you think that there was a handle and hinges.

"How do we open it?" I pressed my hands against the stone etched door, working my fingers along the edges.

"I don't know," Bres said. "Keep trying."

I pushed on the doorway. But it was stone, and had no way to open.

Magic is about willing things to happen, I

thought to myself. That's what Cora kept telling me.

I closed my eyes and called up my power, feeling it crawl through me again and I realized that Card's power was as uncertain of me as I was of it. I coaxed it forward. "A door, we need a proper door to go through."

My hand heated and the stone under my fingers softened, changing. I blinked my eyes and instead of a stone wall with a rectangle line around it, there was a wooden door, hinges, handle and everything.

"Well done, Quinn," Bres kissed me on the cheek, grabbed the handle and pulled the door open, the hinges swinging on frame with ease. "We've got to keep moving. They'll still come after us," he said.

"Are you serious? How?"

"One at a time through the door." His eyes were grim. Double shit. "So it will slow them, but they will still come. Chaos wants you dead."

We stepped through the door and into a pitch-black room —or at least I had supposed it was a room. It could have been the interior of the mountain, or any number of places.

"The next thing was crossing the vale. Which is

a valley, right?" I asked. I started to lift my hand to light a flame for visibility, then stopped. "Maybe you'd better light the fire this time."

A bloom of orange lit over his hand in a perfect round orb and guided us through what turned out to be a valley, indeed, black as a moonless night. If it hadn't been for Bres's fire, we would have been lost completely in the darkness.

"We should still run," he said, his fingers tightening on mine.

"Lead the way."

Breaking into an uneven jog, we moved as fast as we could. There were no pitfalls, no booby traps, but we were waiting for them, expecting them.

The darkness didn't fade. It was just suddenly gone, leaving us blinded by the brilliant sunshine. Which was the first clue something was up.

"Damn it," I said, shading my eyes. I could see nothing past the bright spots that danced in my vision.

Tightening my hand on Bres's, I stepped forward and immediately began to slide. Downhill, on loose shale that skittered under my feet, giving me no purchase.

"Quinn, don't let go!" Bres shouted. The rocks

around us slid and screeched as they avalanched with us, our bodies yanked this way and that. His fingers slipped from mine as my vision came back.

It was as if we were tobogganing down the mountainside, only it was our bodies skimming on the sheets of shale rock instead of a toboggan. As if getting battered by rock and scree wasn't bad enough, at the bottom of the slide waited another group of Fomorii.

How the hell had they beaten us here? Or had there been two groups?

It didn't matter. The only thing that mattered was that we had to get past them, there was no other choice. Distracted by the Fomorii, I didn't see the boulder until I hit it and my body flipped over, slamming me hard into the ground. I dug my fingers and heels in, trying desperately to stop my downward rush into the arms of the Fomorii.

Bres was just ahead of me, not having any more luck than I was. We had only a few brief moments before we were caught. There had to be something we could do.

A deep bellow of thunder rippled across the sky and lightning arced through the clouds, high-lighting the army below. Everything seemed to slow down: my heartbeat, the breath escaping between lips, even our downward slide.

We needed to get to the three smiths. Need. I let my magic spill over me again and it was less painful this time as I let it take form. We needed the smiths.

The magic blitzed out of me, swirling around us in a spinning flurry like a little tornado.

There was a brief flash of gold and a lithe body encased in Fomorii armor stepped into view, though she stood well back from our trajectory. Was that Chaos? The helmet covering her head and hair made me uncertain. Would she come to find me now?

"Quinn, there!" Bres pointed toward a mound behind the Fomorii, a mound that hadn't been there only a split second before.

The dirt mound erupted and three screaming men in kilts leaped out from the ground, swinging weapons. The Fomorii army turned and fell on them, as we skidded the final few feet to solid ground.

Blurs of movement were all I could catch as what could only be the three Smiths fighting a path to Bres and me. There were hundreds of Fomorii, and only five of us. There was no way we could take them all. That didn't mean I would give up.

The first Smith to reach us had wild red hair that stuck up every which way, and he swung a mace as if it were an extension of his arm. "Hello, lass, heard you'd be coming our way. Hurry it up now, kill yerself a beastie or two, then let's be gone. We've work to do!"

A Fomorii picked me up from the right side. I put my hand to its head and unleashed a power bolt. Again, I didn't count on the increase in the combined power of mine and Card's abilities.

The Fomorii's head flew from its shoulders and a fountain of black blood spurt out, splattering my face and chest as the body slumped and its hands released me.

The Smith laughed and raised his mace in a salute. "Aye, lassie, now *that's* how to finish off the bastards! Let's do another, shall we?"

With a roar, he dove back into the fray. Bres yanked me out of the Fomorii's death grip and we ran after the Smith, following the bright red and green kilt.

Bres helped clear the path, his sword cutting down those who had once been his people, forcing them back. I tried not to think how it must hurt him to kill his own. I used my bolts of power twice more, clearing off a good number of Fomorii each time. We reached the mound where the three Smiths waited, holding back the rest of the army.

"Hurry, lassie, get you and your beau in ta safety now," said the red-haired Smith.

I turned in time to see the helmeted warrior fling off her helmet. Strawberry blonde hair spun around her face as Chaos snarled and flung a hand toward us. The black tendrils that flew from her fingers struck like the lightning that had danced across the sky. Fomorii that were in the way were killed, but that would give the impression their deaths were quick. The black tendrils hit them and continued on, but where the Fomorii were touched, chaos literally ensued. For some of them, their skin charred, others, their bodies exploded. One even froze like a chunk of stone then crumbled to the ground. I watched as another clawed at the spot where the black tendrils had touched it until it dug a hole in its own belly, eviscerating itself.

Chaos laughed through it all, her face alight with power as she fed on the destruction she caused.

Someone shoved me into the mound and I

barely kept my feet, the horror of what I'd just witnessed having locked up my ability to move.

Bres wasn't in much better shape, and it took all three Smiths prodding us along to get us moving.

"What the hell was that?" Bres asked, his voice shaky. "Her power . . .that cannot be allowed."

"Ach, that damn Chaos. Her powers are nasty that be for sure," One of the Smith's bright green eyes filled my vision. I swallowed the bile that had risen up my throat. She'd killed her own army, for what? Just to scare us? I hated to admit that it had worked, at least on me.

The second Smith lit a torch. "Yup, tat little nutter, she'd be a one scary beech." I took in his appearance, a black and gray tartan, a bald head and kind eyes that I thought might be hazel though it was hard to say for sure in the firelight.

He took my hand, engulfing it in his own. His skin was rough and callused, but warm. Comforting. I could feel the strength in them, though he held my hand lightly. "Don't be worrying now, even Chaos can't be getting troo our wards. There be some places that will always be safety for those who need it."

Their accents were heavy, a mixture between

Irish and Scottish that left me struggling to translate exactly what it was they were saying.

"We be ta tree Smitts, but I supposed you'd already be knowing tat, yeah?" he asked. I gave a nod.

They led us out of the tunnel and into a clearing of a green meadow surrounded by large trees that were none I recognized from the island. Across the way stood a huge log cabin, and off to one side, a shop with an oversized forge and three anvils with tools set about them.

"Welcome ta our humblest abode, lass." All three gave a bow from the waist. The third Smith was the oldest of the bunch, his gray hair bound in a long braid, the look complete with a long gray beard with beads woven into it, and he had bright blue eyes that reminded me a little of Luke's. He was wearing a red on red kilt and a white shirt that had seen better days.

"Thank you," I said. I couldn't help glancing over my shoulder. The mound we'd stepped out of was gone, settled into the ground.

The first Smith, the one with the red hair, stepped forward. "I be Angus, that there with the shiny cap is Wil, and 'ol gray beard there is Paddy."

"I'm Quinn, this is Bres." The men all nodded

to one another, but it was Paddy who stepped forward.

"Let me see that sword of yours, lad. It looks a mite familiar." Bres handed over his sword, the blade still shiny with black blood. Paddy polished it off, inspecting it first one way, then the other.

Angus grunted. "He tinks every sword is one he's made. He be going daft, though he can still swing a vicious right when he feels to be moved to do so."

Paddy glared at Angus, and Wil just laughed. "Egads, how long since we be having guests? Come on, we should show them to ta house. Feed 'em up. Let 'em rest some. Bit of a fight to get here, yeah?"

I was already shaking my head. "No, I'm sorry, we don't have time. We came here for help. I need you to build me a sword that will be able to. . ." I paused, feeling what I was about to say spin through me. I was asking for a sword to kill Ashling. There had been nothing else I'd seen yet that would allow me to free her. No spell, no magic amulet. Nothing.

It hit me in the gut as if I'd been kicked by a mule. Sinking to the ground, the reality swept through me.

To save the world, I *was* going to have to kill my

sister. Just like the prophecy had said. "I don't want to do this." I whispered. "This isn't right."

The three Smiths exchanged knowing glances. Paddy crouched in front of me, the beads in his beard tinkling. "Lass, you need Excalibur for what you be facing. We made tat sword, imbued it wit ta strength of a soul and gave it to Arthur, the last true king, ta rule. But it's been many a year dat it t'was destroyed. I donna think tat we can help you."

Clearing my throat, I put my hands on my folded knees. "I know. That's why I need you to make me a new one. A new blade, just like it."

Paddy's blue eyes lowered and he shook his head slowly. "I don't tink we can, lass. We have many a sword 'ere, good swords, but none wit ta power you be needing."

"I wish to hell we could," Wil said. "But we be missing all ta vitals."

Bres frowned. "What do you need?"

Angus lifted his hands in the air, ceasing the conversation. "This is a talk for ta anvil. Come on, let's have it out now." He turned and headed toward the covered work area, Paddy and Wil following him.

Bres held his hand out to me. "Don't lose faith, Quinn. We aren't done yet."

I managed to give him a smile and wished with all my heart that I could hang onto his words and truly believe them.

Because he was wrong, I was done. No matter how this ended there was no way to save my little sister. If I got the sword made, I had a weapon to kill her. And if I didn't, she'd kill me and the world.

There was no good way out of this that I could see.

10

At the anvil the three smiths faced me and Bres and the quickly laid out the "vitals" as they said. These as it turned out were a list of items that Angus, Wil, and Paddy mostly had to build a sword. Steel, special wood for the handle, leather for the scabbard. They had the basics. Except for a sword like Excalibur, there was a lot more to it than the basics.

"You see, ta most important tings to make a weapon of power like Excalibur are one, ta weapon of a true king of ta Emerald Isle and two, ta soul of one who needs to make recompense for ta sins in their life."

I leaned a hip against the middle anvil, the sharp edge digging into me a bit. "But you said that the last true king was Arthur." They nodded. "So how are we going to get a weapon of his?"

Angus shrugged. "He had a number of tings. His sword, of course, as well as a dagger . . ." He kept talking, but my ears started to ring and all I could hear was the word dagger. My fingers found the handle of *my* dagger at my waist. The bone was smooth and warm, the etching in it and the blade were Celtic. It had power that has saved me more than once. Cora had told me that when I first met her. She had said that it was bonded to me and my family.

Could it be that my grandfather had known what I would need? That the dagger he'd passed down to me was really once Arthur's? Slowly, I pulled it out and laid it on the anvil. "A dagger like this?"

With a gasp and a choke as a unit, the three Smiths went silent. Paddy whispered, "Lass, how did ya get tat?"

"My grandfather gave it to me. Is it . . . was it, Arthur's?"

Paddy lifted it up off the anvil. "Yes, dis was Arthur's." He fingered the blade, turning it in the light. "If it was passed down to ya, troo yer family, then not only was it Arthur's, den you are Arthur's descendant."

I swallowed hard. "What about the last thing? The soul?" I mean really, how did they expect us to find a soul?

"That be more complicated," Paddy said. "No small thing finding us a soul."

Snapping my fingers, I said, "The hall we passed through, the banshee graveyard. Do you think we could find a soul there?"

Angus shook his head. "Not unless it was a queen. Ta banshees do what they're told, so tay aren't really bad. Obedient, not bad."

I looked at Bres, who'd arched an eyebrow and a slow smile crossed his face. "What was it that Fianna gave you when we left, Quinn? Something that she said you'd earned."

My pocket suddenly felt heavy. I hadn't asked what Fianna had given me, but I had no doubt now what it was now in that moment.

Aednat's soul gem.

The small brown bag looked nondescript when I laid it on the anvil, but when I undid the tie and slid the gem onto the tempered steel, the three Smiths gasped. The blue and green stone was all that was left of Aednat's power and maybe a bit of her soul. I wasn't entirely sure. My heart clenched just thinking about her.

"The gods indeed be looking out for ya, Quinn." Angus dropped a big hand onto my shoulder and patted it. "We can build you ta sword you need, a sister to Excalibur. For a price."

Blinking, I stared up at him, not sure if I'd heard correctly. "What?"

"We can do nothing for free. There is always a cost," he said, his voice sad. "I wish it were different, but if we break that law now, our safety here is forfeit, and the sword would be useless do you."

Bres stepped forward, his eyes narrowed. "What kind of cost?"

The three Smiths put their heads together, the low rumble of their voices filling the two-sided shelter as they discussed, though I could make out nothing of their words.

Stepping over to Bres, I slipped my hand into his.

Any idea what they might come up with?

He shook his head. *Not a clue. I didn't even know this was a possibility. If I'd thought it was, I'd have brought some gold with me.*

With a grunt, Angus stepped away from Wil and Paddy. "We've decided tat ta cost will be someting simple. Someting you'd perhaps like to give us. Someting you'd like to be rid of."

I took a deep breath, thinking I was prepared for anything. Wrong again. "Tell me."

"Your mother."

"Huh?" I half grunted.

Angus flushed. "You see, being ta oracle and all, we thought tat she'd like to live here. It's safe and she don't have to be seeing any more prophecies here. And . . ." he half glanced over his shoulder at Wil, who was suspiciously stone faced.

I looked at Wil, really looked at him, and realized that he was a handsome man. His body was fit and muscular, his eyes were gentle and he had a strong jaw line. Then it hit me. My mother *was the oracle.* The one who'd prophesied everything, the one who had seen her daughters killing each other. And she'd had us anyway. It boggled my mind and yet, even with that, everything she'd done and said made ridiculous sense in that context. She'd tried to keep herself distant from us, to keep her from the pain of losing us. Maybe.

Cora's words whispered through me. *She did not give all the prophecies. I gave the first, as I was the oracle before her. She gave the second, after the two of you were born. It was then that she revolted, that she rebelled and did her best to stop loving you girls.*

Cora's words rocked me and I stumbled outside, ignoring Bres's concern. "Why tell me this now?"

I feel that it's the right time.

Standing outside the covered shop, I struggled to grasp this new twist. "Does that mean Ashling or I am next in line?"

You will be the next oracle. It is through the Tuatha blood that the calling is passed.

Just what I needed, another responsibility.

You won't gain it until your mother is very old. You have time before that happens.

Turning, I headed back into the shop. I would deal with the prophecy or oracle business when I had to. At that moment, it wasn't the time.

My eyes met Wil's hazel ones. "Why her?" I asked, not looking at anyone else. Wil cleared his throat.

"Your mama, and I . . ."

Paddy snorted. "He's been in love wit her and she wit him for their whole bloody lives. But her damn interfering mudder, she stopped ta marriage. It soured your mama, made her a bit crazy."

Wil nodded. "Tis true. I love her. Want her here wit me if you'd let her go."

That man could have been my father if things had turned out differently. "I won't force her," I said.

Angus started to laugh. "You won't have to, lass. All right. We'll make ta sword for ya. You send your mama back here and ta deal is done."

They shooed us away into the house, the sounds of bellows and hammers on steel following us. "How long?" I asked.

"As long as it takes." Was the only answer they gave as they set to work.

The interior of their house was cool and clean. I plunked down on one of the sturdy wooden chairs, my thoughts racing. I looked at Bres. "Did you know that my mother was the oracle?"

He shook his head. "No, whenever the oracle came to see my father, it was at night and her face was covered. But I suspected."

Resting my head in my hands, I tried to understand why a woman would have children knowing they would try to kill each other. That was the only part that didn't make sense. Over and over, I turned it in my mind, trying to find the reason why. Because, while I'd told myself we were done,

Darcy was still my mother, and if there was a chance we could reconcile, it might be worth the try. Maybe.

"I'm going outside a minute, I just need to think," I said, pushing my chair back with a loud scrape. Bres poured a mug of tea. "Here, take this with you." The clay mug was heavy, meant for much larger hands than my own.

I lifted it to my lips and the faint taste of fairy honey whispered across my tongue. The ache in my body from the mad dash of flight began to ease within seconds. Clutching my mug, I stepped back outside and went to watch the three Smiths.

The sight was awe-inspiring. They moved as a unit, a well-oiled machine. Paddy held a piece of metal with a huge pair of tongs while Wil and Angus struck it with hammers, one right after the other. The pounding of the metal was rhythmic and steady. Neither Angus nor Wil moved. Paddy made adjustments by shifting the steel on the anvil.

I wanted to talk to Wil, but knew I couldn't interrupt him, not now.

Bres came to stand beside me, putting one hand on the small of my back. "We're almost there, Quinn. Be easy on yourself for a moment. Rest.

The battle we all will face will be here soon enough."

Leaning into his side, I knew he was right. I'd be facing Chaos, Ashling, before I was ready.

Without a word, Bres took my hand and led me away from the three forging smiths. We walked to the edge of the clearing where a well-worn path started. Again, he led, but didn't let go of me.

Along the edge of the path the flowers bloomed, the scent of them filling the air and mingling with the night. I took a deep breath and let it out in a slow sigh. For a moment, maybe I could forget what was coming. I could pretend that this was nothing more than a moment with a man I was falling for.

The path led us to another small clearing, this one more like the banshee bowers. Enclosed, private and peaceful. A bench sat in the middle next to a pond full of colorful darting fish as they fed on the night bugs.

Bres took me over to it and sat me down. "This is a good spot to rest."

I smiled up at him and he ran his finger along the edge of my jaw. Our eyes met and I couldn't look away, captured by his violet gaze. Slowly, inch-by-inch, he leaned into me until our lips touched, and in that moment, the world was all right, the wrongs of it kissed away by him, by Bres.

His arms wrapped around me, the tea mugs forgotten as he claimed my mouth. Tongue delving deep, I could taste the fairy honey on his lips, along with the flavor that was solely him. He slid his hands under my shirt, running his fingers up and down my spine, tracing patterns that made my skin shiver with anticipation.

I pulled back to catch my breath. "Bres, I don't know who. . ."

"Hush, I know you love us both," he said against my lips, pulling me into his lap. "For now, we are both yours. And when the time comes, I will be content that I had this moment, even if it means there are no others."

11

Hours passed as Bres and I lay in the seclusion of the trees, wrapped around one another, dozing between kissing and tasting one another. There was a peace here, not just in that place, but in his arms. Safety was a feeling I'd almost given up on.

The feel of his body against mine was worth every moment of fear on the run to this place, was worth every worry that we wouldn't make it in time. I let my hands wander over the tattoos that had so fascinated me the first time I'd seen them. "Is it always like this with the fae?" I asked softly.

"Like what?" He murmured as he kissed his way along my collarbone.

"Between people? I . . .I've not felt emotions this intense for anyone before." I wanted to bite back the words because of course I didn't want to throw Luke under the bus but it was true. I'd wanted to kiss Luke, I'd have let him have his way with me if given the chance, but this feeling with Bres was more than that.

He lifted his head. "The fae love deeply, fast, and without worry of what the world might think. But it does not come often, so when it happens, it be something special to be cherished."

I smiled and found his mouth with my own, letting his touch and kiss wash away the worries that ate at me.

That I wouldn't be strong enough.

That nothing would turn out right.

Sometime in the middle of the night, Bres stood and pulled his clothes back on. "Come, let me show you some moves with the sword. You'll be needing them when it comes to Chaos."

Basic swordplay was, in theory, easy to understand. But it was not so easy to learn in a single night. Bres settled for showing me how to block effectively.

We used two long sticks and he had me do the

blocks repeatedly, until I felt like the *Karate Kid* with his first lesson.

"Wax on, wax off. I think I get it," I said, smiling up at Bres.

His brow crinkled. "This has nothing to do with wax."

A burst of laughter I couldn't contain rippled out of me. It felt good, and that made me feel guilty for that spurt of happiness. "Never mind. I think I've got it."

"Let's try a basic attack." He slid through the move, making it look easy. Step, step, swing.

I stumbled the first time, and then slowly, my body did as I asked. Over and over, I repeated the movement.

Bres waved his hand. "That is as good as I think we are going to get. Just remember one thing: don't let her in your guard. If you do that, it'll all be over. Don't let her get past your sword. Okay?"

"Got it. Don't let her stab me." Again, I chuckled, the dark humor suiting me for the moment. Bres didn't laugh.

Sitting, he tugged on my hand to sit down with him, back where we'd started in the coolness of the grass. "Stay with me."

Curling up next to him, I wondered how much

longer it would be before the sword was ready. Would the process take days? I wasn't sure we had that much time. I laid my head against his shoulder. What would happen if we made it through this alive, all of us? Would I be able to choose between the two men? If you'd asked me right there, the choice would have been easy, But I knew that seeing Luke would make it harder.

The night drifted around us, and with it, my thoughts wandered in and out of the present, past and future.

The distant hammering was a continuous sound, so when it stopped I sat up with a bolt. I'd fallen asleep in Bres's arms and the night sky had faded to early dawn, the last of the stars winking out above the clearing that we had made our own.

I touched his face gently, waking him. "They've stopped," I whispered, not wanting to break the spell that had stolen us from the world of battles and death for a short time.

Bres sat up and ran his hand through his hair. Giving me a last lingering kiss, he stood, holding his hand out to me. "Let's go see what they've got for you, *lass*."

We made our way down the path, back the way we'd come. The way was lit by the last few fireflies and the faded, distant twinkling of the stars above our heads. I could easily see my mother here, could see her living out her days in this peace and stillness away from the troubles of the world. I only hoped she would come here and not make me give some other form of payment to the Smiths.

As we emerged from the forest, the forge fire was still lit, and its light filled the main clearing like a bonfire. In front of it stood the three Smiths, Angus just ahead of Wil and Paddy. Across his arms lay a sword covered by a white cloth.

"Quinn, daughter of ta oracle. Come forward."

I walked toward him, stopping only a few feet away. This had the feeling of a ceremony, something I didn't want to screw up. "I am here."

"We have forged for you a sword of power. Wield it wit honor and justice, do only ta harm you must and no more. This is the creed of the blade. Carnwennan be the blade's name." He spoke the name as he placed the hilt into my hand and the cover was drawn from it.

The new sword held some of what I'd already had. The hilt that my dagger had borne, bone, nearly white with wear remained the same. That was where the similarities ended. Just above the handle, set into the cross guard of the blade, was Aednat's stone. The gem was inset so that it was showing blue on one side and green on the other. The actual length of the sword was just the right length for me, not the massive blades that Luke and Bres carried with them.

I held it lightly, feeling the weight of it, feeling the connection between me and it. Lifting my eyes, I couldn't stop the tears that fell, landing on the blade. This was the weapon I would kill Ashling with, the weapon that Aednat's soul now resided in. Bres came up behind me and circled me with his arms.

"There's still a chance. You have to believe, Quinn," he whispered into my ear. "We have to believe that love will be enough to stop the darkness, or what else is there to fight for?"

Wil stepped forward. "He be right. Don't give up. Not on love. Your mama, she had you and Ashling because she believed in ta prophecy and knew it needed to come to pass if our worlds would be mended. She laid her heart on ta altar of sacrifice to save ta world. Can you do any less?"

My throat closed. I knew he spoke true and it shamed me to know how Darcy had been forced to give up her own dreams and the love of a man who cared for her to fulfill a stupid prophecy.

"No, I won't do any less," I said.

It was Paddy's turn. He came forward with a belt and scabbard. "Here you go. Put this on. When ta blade's gem shows blue, you'll be cloaked in shadow, unseen by friend or foe. Pull ta blade and the shadow will be lifted."

He cinched the belt around my waist, helping me adjust it. Turning the blade so the green gem winked outwards, I slid it into the scabbard.

"Thank you," I said, running my hand over the hilt. God above and hell below, how was I going to do this? How was I going to kill Ashling, even if it was just her body? A shaking started in my limbs that I could barely contain. The closer I got to the moment that I would have to face her, the more the reality set in.

Wil took my hand and slipped a ring over my right thumb. "Give this to Darcy. She'll know what it means."

I nodded. "Of course."

On an impulse, I hugged each one of the three Smiths, catching them by surprise. Angus cleared his throat as I stepped back. "Well, then, I guess we'd best be seeing you two off. Come on to ta stables 'round back. There's no way you'll get past that army wit out a little speed. We got just the wee beasties for you."

Leading the way, Angus marched to the back of the house where indeed there was a stable like any other. The creatures inside, however, were another matter altogether. No mere horses waited for us.

They *looked* to be two large black horses, but they had fangs and their eyes were more like a cat's with a vertical slit that narrowed as we came into sight. Two sets of ears pinned backward as we drew closer.

"They're mean bastards," Paddy said. "But they be fast, and they'll kill anyting tat is in your way."

"What are they?" I asked.

Bres answered me. "Aughisky. I thought they were all dead, died out in the last great battle between Fomorii and Tuatha. They're like the kelpie only more vicious. I don't know that this is a good idea." His tone was enough to make me back away from the big black beasts.

Angus let out a breath. "Phaw, don't be a sissy, boy. These two know their lives depend on coming back here. It's ta only safe haven tat they have. Right, my lads?" He swatted one on the rump.

It turned its head and bared its teeth, letting out a low growl. Definitely not a horse sound.

Angus and Wil ignored the growls and saddled up the two Aughisky. Bres pulled me aside and whispered in my ear, "If we get anywhere close to salt water, I want you to throw yourself from its back."

"What? Why?" I asked as he pulled me a little farther away, his face grim.

"They drown their riders and eat them." He said.

"Then maybe we shouldn't be doing this!" I said, feeling a wave of panic. "And I haven't ridden a horse in years. How am I going to stay on if we're riding full tilt to stay ahead of the Fomorii?"

I didn't have time to ask any more questions. Wil grabbed me about the waist and swung me up onto the back of the first Aughisky, ignoring my squeak of protest.

There were no reins, only the slick black mane that felt reminiscent of seaweed. I gripped the hair until my knuckles were white and took a deep breath. The beast trembled below me, its sides shivering as if flies were landing on its hide.

Bres mounted the other Aughisky as if he'd been born to the saddle and not the water.

Angus patted my leg. "Don't worry, lass, these two boys will get you past ta Fomorii, wit out a doubt. You only have ta tell them where it is you want ta go."

Licking my lips, I nodded. "Nuadha has a camp somewhere on the island." I glanced at Bres who gave me a small nod. "So we'll have to go to Fianna first to find out where Nuadha is. Unless you know?"

The three Smiths shook their heads in unison. "Nope, to ta banshee queen it is, then, boys, then you'll take Quinn and Bres ta their next destination, then come straight back home. No hunting."

The Aughisky below me let out a snort and Bres's mount actually chuckled. This was seeming like less and less of a good idea.

Before I could say anything else, Angus slapped the rump of my Aughisky and we bolted out of the stable, Bres and his mount hot on our heels. I gripped the mane as tightly as I could, feeling the strands slide through my fingers. I had to settle for gripping the front edge of the saddle.

The Aughisky was smooth, its gait was one that was easy to sit, but the speed was terrifying. The trees blurred by, which was bad enough, but when the mound we'd entered through rose as if it were a living thing and opened, the creatures we rode *dove* into it. I couldn't stop the scream that escaped me. Hunching over the saddle, I buried my face against the neck of the Aughisky, wishing to be on my own two feet as soon as possible. The scent of the ocean surrounded me, and I actually looked up expecting to see water.

But there was no water, only the exit out of the mound into the base of the ravine where the Fomorii army waited for us.

We burst out of the mound, startling the Fomorii guards. My mount struck out with its fanged mouth, snatching a pound or two of flesh as it ripped by the Fomorii. From the squeal behind me, I had no doubt that Bres's mount had done a follow up bite.

Splatters of blood flipped back toward me as the Aughisky threw its head back to swallow the chunk of flesh. Flesh eating horses were not my idea of a good, safe ride, not that I had any choice now. "Please don't eat me." I whispered.

The Fomorii were in an uproar as they scrambled to stop us, like we'd kicked an anthill good, but they were too late. We were already climbing the shale hill, covering it with a speed that left the army in the dust. At the top, I yelled, "Stop!" and, remarkably, my mount froze, obeying my command.

Bres and his mount had caught up to us. I stared back the way we'd come, my eyes searching for a sign of the strawberry blonde curls that would give Chaos away. But there was nothing. She'd gone to ground.

In a burst of anger, I screamed across at the Fomorii. "Tell Chaos she is DEAD!"

My mount gave a snort and I was fairly certain he approved. "Let's go." Leaping forward, the Aughisky ran, retracing our footsteps back the way we'd come, bursting through the waterfall and covering the Hall of the Dead in no time. Bres kept trying to get my attention, to get me to speak to him, but I was buried in my own thoughts and wanted to stay there.

So much to do, with each moment taking us closer to a battle I did not want.

It wasn't long before we were at the edge of Cathedral Grove, the banshees' Enchanted Forest. The Aughisky slowed their mad pace to a simple lope, and the world no longer was blurred around us. We weren't stopped by the banshee guards, but we were followed as we made our way deep into the forest to find Fianna.

We didn't dismount, which I was glad for. I didn't think I'd ever be able to walk again. The muscles in my legs and butt were aching, and I was certain I had a blister on my ass despite the smooth movement of my mount.

Fianna raised a hand in greeting to us and we shared our request. "Nuadha has chosen to camp on the far side of the island where the ocean meets the shore. We cannot go with you now, but when the time comes for the battle between you and Chaos, the banshees will be there. We stand with you, Quinn."

The Aughisky spun on their haunches and I shouted my farewells. This was going to be a long ride, even at the speed that our mounts could manage.

Quinn, love, talk to me. Bres's words whispered across my mind and I finally relented, letting him in.

I have to do it. This is the weapon I'll use to take her head. And I am terrified that I won't be able to do it. And terrified that I will. The words were painful as the scabbard bounced against my thigh reminding me of the weapon made for one purpose.

I glanced at Bres, his face pale with the shock of my words. *You don't know that.*

Turning my face into the wind, I hunched over the saddle, the hilt of Carnwennan digging into my side. The problem was while I wanted to believe I could save Ashling, everything was pointing to her death being the only way to save the world. How could I tell people I gave up the world for a single life? Even if that life was the whole world to me?

12

Both Aughisky did what the three Smiths said they would. They ran at a speed that no one could match, taking us all the way to the west coast in under an hour. It was early morning, and dawn was breaking through the cloudy skies when we approached the shore of the pacific ocean. The scent of the water reached me and my mount at the same time. His head came up and his nostrils flared, ears pricking forward as he gave a little grunt. His steps faltered for the first time.

"Quinn, dismount. Right now," Bres said, his words brooking no argument. "Now!"

But my body was sluggish after the time in the

saddle and it didn't want to obey me. My mount snorted and spoke, shocking the hell out of me.

"Lady of the Sea, dismount. I cannot contain my urge to take to the water much longer." He grumbled. "And I would not take you under the waves if I can avoid it."

I slid off, my knees buckling when my feet touched the ground, but it was enough that I was no longer in the saddle. The two Aughisky bolted toward the water, bucking and tearing the saddles from each other's backs. We watched as they dove into the water, their sleek black bodies diving down, disappearing under the waves in a few short leaps.

"Thank you," I said, knowing they couldn't hear me, but saying it anyway. Letting out a groan, I tried to stand. "I'm so sore, everything hurts."

Bres chuckled, mimicking the three Smiths. "Ah, it weren't so bad, lass."

I took a swat at him, though it was only half-hearted. "Don't tease. We have to find Nuadha and I'm walking like an old lady."

He took my hand and as we turned from the ocean the sound of multiple swords being drawn from their scabbards cut across the rush of water on the sand. Bres spun, pulling his sword, barely in time to parry what would have been a fatal blow. The blades clashed and the sound of steel on steel cracked the morning air open.

"Put down your weapons, Fomorii!" our attacker cried as he took another swing that Bres easily parried. His armor was polished to a sheen and reflected the weak light of the morning in bright flashes.

"Stop it, we aren't with Chaos!" I yelled, foolishly thinking that they would listen. Others slipped up behind us, weapons drawn. I couldn't fend them off, and if Bres tried he'd be killed, I was sure of it. I did the only thing I could think of—I flipped a barrier over Bres and me, protecting us from the men who'd surrounded us.

They circled around, testing the barrier, slashing at it with their weapons. Trying to push their way in. But my power was more than doubled with what I'd taken from Card and the steel of their swords bounced off uselessly.

"Drop your barrier, Quinn," I recognized that voice, but not because I'd ever met him in person. Slowly, I turned to face Nuadha, leader of the Tuatha de Daanan. His hair was shorn, not the

long silver braid it had been at his battle with
Balor where he'd cursed the Fomorii. I'd heard his
voice then, and I knew it clearly.

"Nuadha, we aren't here to fight. We're here to
help," I said.

Keep her from Nuadha. My father's request of
Balor rumbled through me and I had no doubt
that we—I—was in deep shit.

"Then drop the barrier." His eyes showed no
warmth nor malice.

A glance over my shoulder to Bres for some
sort of indication of what we should do only gave
me a half shoulder shrug to go on. *I don't know,
Quinn.* His words were soft inside my mind.

Damn. Where was Cora now when I could
truly use her advice? Nowhere. I couldn't even feel
her. A hitch in my throat caught me. Now? She
abandoned me, now?

I dropped the barrier. "You see, we are on your
side . . ." The men swarmed over Bres, but when I
went to aid him, he shook his head. "No, it's what I
expected."

Nuadha strolled up beside me. "He is a traitor,
two times over. Why would you protect him?"

I frowned up at the silver-haired man. He was
everything Luke had been when I'd first met him,

arrogant and cocky, only compounded by years of truly believing he was the best that the Tuatha had to offer.

"I trust him with all my heart," I said.

The men around us laughed as if I'd said something dirty. Nuadha just grunted. "Take him to the stocks. The council will deal with him after the battle."

He grabbed me by the arm, his fingers tightening painfully around my bicep. "And you, Quinn, what are we to do with you?" He yanked me alongside himself as if I were a child. I jerked backward, forcing him to let me go or get in a tug of war.

"I am here to help you stop Chaos. That's it. You can keep your stupid leadership spot. I sure as hell don't want it," I snapped.

His lip started to curl up, but it stopped midrise. "Again, I believe we shall let the council deal with you." He gave a sharp whistle. "Guards, take her to the stocks with her pet Fomorii."

Three guards rushed me and I didn't know what to do. These were supposed to be the good guys, the ones who stood with me as I faced down Chaos.

Bres tried to calm me. *Don't fight them, Quinn.*

Luke will get us out. They don't call him the Charmer for nothing.

His words didn't soothe my anger, but they kept me from lashing out, which would have been a disaster with the strength of not only my power, but Card's too.

They hauled us down the beach, over a sand dune and into the sparse edge of the forest. Carnwennan was taken from me, but I wasn't too worried. I could feel the bond with my sword even more strongly than I had when it was only a dagger. I had no doubt I could call the weapon to my hand when I needed to.

We were tossed onto a rough patch of dirt and sand. Individual barriers were put around us, each with our own guards and then we were left there.

"Well, ain't this a kick in the ass," I muttered. So much for being the Chosen One.

I looked at Bres, who just smiled. "This isn't my first time to be in trouble with Nuadha. He'll come around. He always does."

Laughing, I said, "Somehow it doesn't surprise me that this isn't your first time."

He leaned back against the barrier, his eyes sparkling with devilry. "First time with you."

Heat rushed up my face and I shook my head. Flirting at a time like this when our heads could end up on pikes? What was wrong with us? Then again, maybe that was why, because if there is nothing left to lose, that was when you saw the truth.

The guards turned their backs to us, taking their watch seriously. Of course, I took the opportunity to call Carnwennan to me the moment they turned. For a moment I worried that the sword wouldn't be able to go through the barrier, but a split second later it appeared, glittering steel in the sun.

The sword handle was warm in my palm and I laid the weapon at my feet and buried it under a thin layer of sand. No need to show the Tuatha that I had my weapon back.

The sun continued to rise, and the heat in my barrier increased faster than it should have, as if I was in a hot house and not just sitting on the sandy beach. By noon, I was panting and the sweat ran down my body soaking my clothes. The need for water was beyond anything I'd previously experienced.

Torture it was to be then? This was not

warming me to Nuadha if he thought this was the way to treat anyone.

A thought trickled through my mind like the water I so desperately craved. Reaching out with my senses and Card's power, I found a seam of clear water deep below me. Calling it upward, I coaxed the fresh water into my prison until I had a bubbling spring I could drink from. I cupped it up to my mouth. The water was cold, a bit gritty from coming through the sand, and the best thing I'd ever drunk in my life.

Drinking my fill, I splashed the icy cold water over my face, the back of my neck and chest. My guard glanced at me once, frowned, and then looked away. All the better. Now for Bres. Pulling on the water again, I coaxed and cajoled it into rising below Bres, creating a spring for him.

His eyes widened. I gave him a nod. At least we wouldn't die of dehydration. Dying of something else, say a sword thrust from Nuadha —that, I wasn't so sure we'd be able to avoid.

Down the beach, I could hear shouting— screaming actually. I rolled to my side, my head propped up on my arm, my fingers resting just over the hilt of Carnwennan. It was the most effort I was willing to make, even for a scuffle.

A petite figure was screaming into Nuadha's face, body cloaked, but obviously feminine. I sat up. Twice she screamed my name, asking where I was, and what had been done to me.

"Mom?" Her hood slipped back revealing the curls both Ashling and I had inherited. I stood. "MOM!"

She spun, saw me and started to run across the sand. Even at this distance, I could see tears tracking down her face.

Nuadha yelled at her to stop, but she didn't listen. I had a split second to see and understand what was about to happen. Nuadha raised his hand with power circling around him as he prepped a power bolt.

I had a choice to make. Save my mom, or let him kill her.

There was no choice really. I called Carnwennan to my hand, sliced through the barrier and ran toward Darcy. "Get down!" I yelled. The glint in Nuadha's eye told me everything. This was a setup. Darcy dropped to the ground as Nuadha's power bolt skimmed over her head and came straight at me.

With everything I had, using my power the strength of Card's power I threw a flat barrier up.

Nuadha's power bolt slammed into it with a sound of thunder booming, but it didn't break through. Instead it bounced the bolt meant to cause my death back toward a wide-eyed Nuadha. He dropped to the ground, the bolt whipping out past him and into the ocean with a tremendous thump of water and air.

Running to my mom's side, I helped her stand. "What are you doing here?"

"Looking for you. The visions, they've changed," she whispered. "There is a chance you can still save Ashling. I never thought it possible, but there is a chance."

Her eyes were as wide and as sincere as I'd ever seen them.

Nuadha broke the moment. "Traitor! Give me that sword!" I could see the hunger, a lust even, in his eyes as he stared at Carnwennan and I stepped back, taking my mother with me. "Nope, can't do that. It's mine."

He snarled, "Give it to me now!"

Darcy and I scrambled back, Nuadha following us step by step. I didn't want to fight him. I knew I couldn't win on skill alone, and I was pretty sure I'd kill him if I just used my powers. I was strong, but I had no real control or finesse over my abilities.

"Nuadha, stand down!" An older man stepped into sight, Luke at his side. I couldn't stop the grin that split my face when I saw him. He gave me a salute and a wink.

Nuadha froze, a snarl twisting his lips. "Kale. I will not have her take my place."

"I don't want it," I said.

"It's not a choice you or I make!" he roared. His face was mottled red and white with his rage, and he didn't lower his hand.

The man who had stopped him—Kale—shook his head. "Nuadha, this is a decision for the whole council. . . you have let your fear rule you. And that is what will end your time as a leader of the Tuatha De Dannan."

I saw the moment that Nuadha made his decision, saw the calm acceptance that he would end this now one way or another.

Crap, crap, crap. I pushed Darcy down and sprinted toward Bres. Darcy screamed behind me, "Nuadha, no!"

It was the only warning I had. I dropped to the ground as a power bolt sizzled over the top of my head. Leaping to my feet, I made it to Bres and smashed through the barrier with Carnwennan.

Bres shouldered me aside, hollering, "Stay out of the way!" as Nuadha rushed us.

Three strides behind Nuadha was Luke, pulling his sword free of his scabbard. Nuadha glanced over his shoulder. "Good, Luke, keep Bres busy."

He thought Luke was with him but I knew better, and I lowered my weapon.

Nuadha never saw the blow coming. Luke smashed the hilt of his sword into the back of Nuadha's head, dropping him to the ground in an unconscious heap.

"What the hell was that about?" I gasped out, adrenaline coursing through my veins.

Luke snapped his fingers. "Guards, put him in chains. Now." There was no arguing that voice. The power and charm that he put into his words made doubly certain that he was obeyed.

Guards milled about, putting Nuadha into chains as he slowly came to.

Luke stared after Nuadha. "He's been off the whole time I've been back. He's not the leader I remember him to be. His fear has made him dangerous."

Bres shook his head and ran a hand through his hair. "I know what happened to him."

Everyone paused what they were doing, looked to Bres for the understanding of Nuadha's sudden madness.

"Chaos has a hold of him."

13

With Nuadha in chains and in his own little barrier that kept him locked away, we made our way to a tent city the Tuatha had set up. The largest structure in the middle of the makeshift camp belonged to the council and Nuadha. The council member we'd met hushed us all on the way there.

I tried to query Kale as we walked, but the only response I got to my questions was—"We will discuss all behind the walls of the council. Patience young one."

Darcy gripped my hand the whole way, and Bres and Luke stayed right behind us, guarding my back.

As we walked, my hand gripped in Darcy's, I

realized it was the first time in many years she'd willingly taken my hand, or touched me at all.

It's because she is the oracle and her visions one day will cease, and yours will start. That is why she wouldn't touch you, Cora said, surprising the hell out of me.

I thought you had left me, I said, unable to keep the bitterness out of my mind. Cora had kept so much from me, so much that could have helped me understand, and maybe could have stopped some of this hurt and madness.

I can't remember everything anymore, Quinn. It's why I came to you when Ashling and you first came to the West Coast. It's why I'm with you now. I am doing my best with what I have left, even if you don't believe me.

Ah, a punch in the gut would have been preferable to the shame that filled me. *I'm sorry. Why did you keep Wil and Darcy apart?*

I felt her shift as if adjusting herself. *Because he wasn't good enough for her. A smith! She was to be the oracle. She needed a strong man, like Lir, to love her.*

This conversation would take us nowhere. *Okay, fine. Whatever. Tell me about why she wouldn't touch me, hug me, or hold me, even as a child.*

Cora let out a sigh. *Because as you saw in the*

helicopter, her visions can be passed to her offspring, as one or both could become an oracle in their own right. The more she touched you, the more she hugged you the more you'd see when you were still young.

I squeezed Darcy's hand. She looked at me and gave me a half smile. "I'm so sorry," she whispered.

I untangled my hand from hers and slipped Wil's ring off my thumb and pressed it into the palm of her hand. "I understand better now, and while it hurts, I can let some of that go." I took my hand from hers so she could see the ring. "He still loves you."

Everything seemed to shift in that moment. Years were stripped from her, the bitter, selfish woman I knew full of anger and pain was gone, leaving only a woman who looked strikingly like Ashling, young and vulnerable. The resemblance was true, right down to the innocent wide green eyes, and the hope that filled them. "How did you find this . . . I don't understand."

"It's the last thing I'll ever ask of you. Go to him, be happy, that is all there is left." I stopped walking, forcing the others to stop too. I didn't care about the audience as I pulled her into a hug, and she clung to me, crying. Her body shivered as I let go, her eyes squeezed shut as if she were holding back, or more accurately, as if she were in physical pain.

"I was a terrible mother." She whispered. "I loved you both, but I was a terrible mother."

I answered simply. "Yes. But I think I understand why. I don't know what I'd be like if you forced me away from the man I loved and made me bear another's child, not once, but twice."

Cora shifted again inside me, and the wash of shame I felt was not my own.

"It was for the prophecy. I knew it had to be done. I just couldn't love you two girls like you should have been, not knowing what was coming, not knowing I'd lose at least one of you, and maybe both," she whispered.

I shrugged. "It's made both of us stronger. Which is what we need now."

We stepped inside the council's tent to see Nuadha chained to a chair in the middle. He was just starting to come around, his head lolling from side to side.

The council of twelve, six men and six women, were huddled together in the far back of the tent. Surprisingly, my mother strode to the front of the room and raised her hand for silence. "I will speak, and you will listen. I have shirked my duties as oracle for far too long. Nuadha has been spelled by Chaos and she has warped his mind."

She crouched in front of Nuadha and beckoned me closer. He was blinking up at her and she tipped his head backward, her fingers trembling, a bead of sweat sliding down the side of her face. "Do you see that there, Quinn?" A dark spot was growing on the corner of his eye, not unlike the blackness I'd seen in Ashling's eyes, and I said so.

"Yes, it is the mark of Chaos. Search the troops. There can be none with this mark left to roam free. They should not be harmed, but they cannot be allowed to cause harm," she said.

The council leapt to her command, again surprising me. They filed out, almost running to do her bidding. "They used to listen to my mother like that," Darcy said softly. She swallowed hard and wiped her hand over her face, brushing away the sweat on her skin. "Until she no longer gave them the visions. Then they cast her aside."

We stood, Darcy, Bres, Luke and I, alone in the tent with Nuadha, who was fully recovered. There was shouting outside, the clash of men and metal. How many had already been taken by Chaos?

"Should we make a barrier?" I asked.

Both boys went to the door and stepped

outside. I could hear them discussing the situation and trusted they would make a good call. I crouched in front of Nuadha. "Do you know why you are tied up? Do you understand that Chaos is making you do these things to split apart the Tuatha?"

He snorted and spit at my feet. "There is no such thing as Chaos, a boogeyman of the old gods. Your sister has spoken to me in a dream. She told me that she has taken the throne of the Fomorii from her father and she wants to join with the Tuatha, just as the prophecy has foretold."

Darcy asked. "And what of the great evil that must be overcome, hmm? How did she explain that?"

His head bobbed. "She told me that a woman claiming to be the Chosen One would ride into camp on the back of an Aughisky, and so you did. She is the oracle now." He glared at me.

"What has that got to do with anything?" I asked, before I realized what he was implying. "You think I'm the evil that needs to be destroyed?"

He nodded, his eyes glittering with hatred.

Darcy put her hand on my arm. "You will not be able to convince him of anything, not while

Chaos holds him in sway. But there may be a way to save Ashling, Quinn."

"Tell me."

"You have to offer yourself to Chaos, make a trade. She will take it believing that you have the better power for her to use."

I nodded. That made sense. "But how will I fend her off? I saw how she devoured Ashling, and she's as strong as I am."

Darcy shook her head. "No, she's not. She was always the weaker one, she let fear rule her from a young age." She shuddered and her body crumpled to the floor. Lying there, she sobbed out, "I am sorry, I've tried to fight this."

"Mom, what's wrong?" I bent to help her, wrapping my arms around her middle and sitting her up.

Her eyes rolled in her head and she let out a short gasp. "Don't listen to me, she's so strong, I can't keep her at bay any longer. Tie me up."

Luke and Bres rushed back into the room.

"What happened?" Luke asked.

"I don't know. She was telling me how I might be able to stop Chaos and save Ashling and then she just started to shudder," I smoothed her hair back so I could see her face. Her eyelids fluttered and I pulled my hand away, then pressed it to her face, opening her left eyelid.

There, next to the center of her eye, was a dark spot.

The mark of Chaos.

14

My mother had the mark of Chaos in her eye. She was under that monster's control now.

She started to scream and I held her down at the shoulders, then flipped her over onto her stomach. "Bres, help me tie her. She's got the mark."

"Strange that she showed it to us, don't you think? That she told us how to see it in the others?" Luke asked, he crouched beside her and held her shoulders to the ground. His voice got soft and I wasn't sure if he was talking to me, or if he was speaking his thoughts out loud. "She looks so much like Ashling, even her eyes."

"She was trying to fight back. I thought maybe

she was sick, or hurt," I said. I looked at Bres. "It was right after I gave her the ring from Wil. I think that hope gave her the strength to fight Chaos off for a few minutes."

Luke gave a *huh?* which I chose to ignore. We didn't have time to re-hash my mother's sad love life and where it might end up.

As we finished tying her up, the council filed back in, minus three members. "We have them all rounded up," Kale said, the one who seemed to be the speaker, announced. Then his mouth dropped upon seeing Darcy tied on the floor.

"Not the oracle too! Gods have mercy on us if Chaos has taken her too!"

"Yes, though I believe she was trying to fight for us, showing us the mark, telling us how to see it," I said. I let out a deep breath, bending at the waist, my hands on my knees. Bres put his hand on my lower back.

"Just breathe, Quinn. You can do this, love."

The silence in the room took me a minute to absorb. They were waiting on me to lead them. Well, crap.

"Okay, put all those with the mark somewhere safe. When Chaos is defeated, I think the mark should go with her," I said, hoping I was right. I picked out two of the younger-looking council members and sent them to do that. Guards came and moved a screaming, ranting Nuadha and a sullen but quiet Darcy.

When they were gone, silence again reigned. I licked my lips. "Tell me what you know so far."

What came next was so very much worse than I could have expected.

Chaos had been as busy as I had been, putting the world into a tailspin of destruction. Natural disasters had ravaged all the continents. Hurricanes, earthquakes, tsunamis, and every imaginable force of nature had been unleashed on the world in the space of only a few days.

The human world was in an upheaval as the world of the fae prepared to face Chaos one last time.

"How many have been killed?" I whispered.

"Hundreds of thousands. The death toll is rising every day. The humans are calling it the apocalypse," one of the council members said. "They are waiting for a savior, but their governments have failed them, and more and more people are dying each day."

Suddenly the quiet of Cathedral Grove, the

lack of vehicles and people that I'd taken note of but not really considered sunk in.

The world seemed to tilt under my feet. Bres slipped an arm around my waist, and Luke touched my arm, but wouldn't even take my hand. "You couldn't have stopped this any sooner," he said, his blue eyes holding my gaze. "Don't you dare think this is your fault. Its not."

Bres tightened his arm around me. "He's right. This be her doing, not yours."

The council members said nothing, their faces left carefully blank. No doubt they were used to dealing with Nuadha, which said a great deal about their reaction to the situation. How long had Chaos been leading Nuadha by the nose? How long had they been forced to do what she wanted through his bidding?

"I need...a moment." I pointed to the council. "Leave us here, return in an hour. Please."

They filed out, obedient without question. Not a good thing in a council that was there to advise a leader.

"Chaos has been running things for a while, I think," I said. "Look at how they are reacting to me, as if I'm about to fly off the handle and order that their heads be struck off."

Luke grimaced. "I bet that's why Nuadha and the council forbade me from coming after you. Chaos was already in control then. She was already laying her plans. Not free yet, but laying the groundwork."

"Good thing you disobeyed them." I attempted a smile, though inside, my heart was breaking. So many people had died because of Chaos — because I hadn't stopped her fast enough. Because I was afraid of what was coming.

Bres dropped his forehead to my shoulder. "It was my pa who did this."

"He did and didn't," I said. "I've no doubt Chaos has been planning this for a long time. She's been putting all her pawns into place. Don't you remember what Fianna said? Aednat had been swayed by Chaos years ago, even while she was locked away. Now it's up to us to stop her. That's all there is to it."

I stepped away from the two boys, my thoughts racing. "Do you think Chaos will meet me in open battle?"

Both of them shook their heads. Luke answered first. "No, not a chance. Not now that you have Carnwennan you are even more dangerous to her." He motioned to the sword at my hip. "She'll know it is the one thing that can destroy her, and you are prophesied to do just that."

Bres nodded his agreement. "It's too great a chance that she'll lose to you. I think she'll try to kill you from a distance, use assassins and such to get close to you."

My blood chilled at what they were saying. We were in a full-blown war, and the survival of not only the fae, but the human world rested squarely on me. I drew a slow breath and pushed the fear and desire to curl up in a corner and close my eyes away. "Then we have to find a way to draw her out, to trick her into meeting me." I refused to think about the reality of what I was saying, of what it would mean when I did face her.

Death for one of us, maybe even both.

Luke folded his arms. "Do you have something in mind?"

I thought for a moment, my brain rolling over the possibilities. "What if we used Nuadha? We could set him free." Luke sucked in a sharp breath, but Bres just watched me quietly, letting me talk. "We could use him to draw her here. If she thinks she has an ally in Nuadha, she won't hide from him."

Bres began to pace. "It might work. If we had

someone in camp who could report back to us about her movements, we could find someone who could influence Nuadha." He glanced at Luke. "You could do it. We'd be able to trust you, and you've always been able to bend Nuadha to your way of thinking, even when he's been opposed."

Tapping his fingers on the edge of a chair, Luke nodded. "Yes, that would work. You and Quinn could wait just outside of the army's camp for my signal."

I lifted my hands. "Whoa, I wasn't thinking of leaving Luke behind. I was thinking someone else could do this, one of the council members maybe." That sounded feeble even to me. But I didn't want to put him into danger, not after I'd only just brought him back from the dead.

Luke smiled. "Who else would you trust?"

"What if she figures out that you're on our side?" I whispered, thinking of the black tendrils that had devoured the Fomorii, her own army. I started to shake. "I can't lose you again." I looked to Bres. "Either of you. There has to be another way then sending Luke into Chaos's circle."

Though we spent the next hour working through different scenarios, none worked as well as the first. I fought the two boys on it, in spite of the fact that it had been my idea at first, but in my heart I knew it was the only chance we had to get close to her.

In the end, the plan was to set Nuadha free that night before any suspicion could be roused.

When the council came back, I informed them that we would have an answer for them in the morning. They left as quickly as they'd come, seemingly happy to be out of the presence of their new "leader." Did they fear me, or did they think I was going to end up getting killed so they didn't want to get to know me? I guess it didn't really matter at that point.

We had several hours before it was even dark, and both Bres and Luke insisted that I try to rest while they readied the plan. After the ride in on the Aughisky, and the time spent in the scorching hot barrier, I didn't argue. I wanted to sleep, wanted to escape this mad world I'd been tossed into.

I was shown to a darkened tent where a bed and clean clothes were laid out for me. The basin of hot, soapy water that waited for me was pure heaven. I stripped out of my jeans and T-shirt and scrubbed far too many days' worth of dirt, fear, and blood off my body. I scrubbed until my skin tingled and the water in the basin was dark, the suds gone.

Slipping into the clean clothes, I wondered at how well they would fit. Snug khaki-colored pants that tucked into a pair of leather knee-high boots, and a white blouse that was nearly see-through, clung to me as if tailored for my body. If it hadn't been for the camisole, it would have been indecent. Fully dressed, with Carnwennan in its sheath and strapped to my hip, I lay down, sleep claiming me instantly.

I should have known that it would be far from restful, and maybe a part of me had hoped to see her here.

"Quinn, please, I don't have much time." I opened my eyes to Ashling leaning over me in the same white dress as before, her eyes full of fear. It was a dream, but it felt real. Maybe it was.

"Ash." I pulled her into my arms and hugged her to me, feeling how frail her body had become as if she were wasting away.

"I can't help you, there is nothing I can do, but I wanted to see you again, one last time," she whispered into my hair.

"Don't say that." My words caught in my throat.

"We are not saying goodbye. That isn't how our story ends. It's not over yet."

She started to cry and I rocked her like I had when we were younger, and she'd been afraid of the dark. "Ash, we can get through this, just like everything else."

"Don't lie to me," she said, pulling back so she could look me in the face. "I know you had a sword made, one that would kill Chaos. I'm not angry. I understand, but don't lie to me."

I closed my eyes, tears spilling down my cheeks. "I don't know if I can do it."

She grabbed my shoulders and shook me. "You are the strongest person I know, Quinn. You are my hero, the one person I look up to. Don't let me down. Don't let her win, the world doesn't deserve her."

I put my hands over hers. "Do you remember when we used to wonder about Mom, if there had ever been someone she really loved?"

The change in subject caught her off guard. I told her about Wil, about how Cora forced Darcy to produce a child with Lir, and then Balor, and how Wil was still waiting for her. About how he'd given me a ring to give to mom so she could find her way back to him.

"I think you'd like him. There's something about him that seems so calm, so easy to just be yourself," I said. Ashling was sitting beside me, our arms around each other. "It's amazing to think he's waited all this time for her. Which I guess means that it was real all along."

"Love makes us do crazy things," she whispered. "I think I'm falling in love with someone, but I can't tell him that. Not now, not knowing what is coming. But it doesn't stop me from going to him as often as I can, just to talk to him. I think he feels something for me too."

Her confession surprised and cut into me at the same time. Ash deserved a chance to have a shot at love, to find out all about what that meant, how it felt to love someone with all her heart and have that given back to her tenfold. It hurt a little, jealousy rearing its head, that she would spend whatever time with this new man in her life rather than me, but I did understand. Just the thought of leaving the two men I cared deeply for made my own heart ache with enough pain to steal my breath.

"Yes, love does make you do crazy things," I said, holding her tightly as if that would keep her here with me.

She looked up at me, pinned me with her gaze. "Don't let it make you do anything crazy, Quinn. You can't change this path we're on. I know you love me, but this is the way it's going to be." Ashling flinched as though she'd been hit. I frowned and tucked a strand of her hair behind her ear. "What's wrong?"

"I have to go." She kissed me on the cheek. "Be brave, Quinn. She will try to trick you, she will try to use me against you, just be brave and do what you must. Okay? And tell him I love him . . . after I'm gone."

Her image shimmered, and I was left alone in the tent. A hand on my shoulder brought me fully out of the dream. Bres leaned over me. "Everything's ready. It's time to go."

I sat up and rubbed my hands over my face. Ashling was fading. We were running out of time. I nodded and took his hand, clinging to him for strength. "Let's do this."

15

Bres led me away from the tent and away from the main encampment of the Tuatha. Creeping along we moved in silence until he and I were alone behind a sand dune about a half mile from camp. The nearly full moon was high overhead and the night was clear of any cloud cover which meant we could see clearly for a long stretch of the beach.

"Do you think it went okay?" I asked for probably the tenth time.

He didn't get upset, just took my hand and lifted it to his lips. "Luke is a fighter. He knows what he's doing, Quinn. We can trust him."

We lay on our bellies looking toward the Tuatha camp. The fires were burning high, which we could just see at this distance. Suddenly a great shout went up from a series of guards, and I knew that Luke had released Nuadha and all those taken by Chaos's mark. One of the last things we'd decided was to let them all go. Trying to keep that many prisoners while fighting was a good way to get sandwiched between enemies.

The plan was that Luke would tell Nuadha that he'd never believed in me, not once he saw how weak I was and that my blocking of the power bolt meant to kill me was a fluke, or maybe someone else had put it up. Both Bres and Luke thought the Tuatha leader would buy it, not seeing past his own arrogance and the control that Chaos had on him.

There was a lot of movement in the camp and then silence. The stillness was broken by a great crashing of drums, and then we could hear someone shouting. I couldn't make out the words or the voice, only that it was a man.

"That's Nuadha," Bres said. "But I can't make out what he's saying."

I strained to catch a word, phrase, anything, but we were just too far away. "Should we get closer?"

Bres shook his head. "No. Luke said he would

talk to Nuadha about bringing Ashling...Chaos here. We have to be patient."

A part of me wanted everything to just hurry up and get on with it. I had to face her. That wasn't in doubt, but the waiting was torture, my stomach in knots and my body on the cusp of adrenaline overload.

Suddenly there was a burst of flame and the clash of swords. I sat up and strained my eyes. "That's Luke's fire," I said. "He shouldn't be fighting. Not unless . . ."

"Shit," Bres said, scrambling to his feet. "Nuadha didn't fall for it." He pointed to two figures battling across the night sands, out into the waves. I saw Nuadha lift his blade, saw him disarm Luke. No. I couldn't let this happen!

I beckoned the water into a wave and it crashed into the two men. It saved Luke, but only for a moment. Seconds later, a figure walked out into the water and plucked Luke up. Darcy held him up as if he were a wet rag doll. I heard her words as if she were standing next to me.

I'd seen this . . .after the helicopter crash what seemed like a lifetime ago. There had been a moment when Luke was helping Darcy out of the water that their positions had changed, superimposing over one another and Darcy had been holding Luke, just like she was now.

"She will come to Chaos if we hold his life on the line. She loves him. He's the perfect hostage to draw her out."

My heart clenched. "No." What had we done?

Bres pulled me down onto my belly. I hadn't ever realized I'd started to stand. "Don't do anything. They won't kill him. We can figure this out, Quinn."

A soft scuffle of bush behind us spun us both around. Skulking toward us was the humped back shape of a Fomorii. With its head down, eyes toward the ground, it lifted its hands in shaky supplication. "I mean no harm. I come in peace. Please, we need to be free of her. She is not Fomorii any longer. Bres, you know this. You know what she is."

I'd pulled out Carnwennan and steadied myself on the sloping sand as the Fomorii spoke. "How do I know you tell me the truth? Why shouldn't I make sure there is one less of you on the battlefield?"

Now it did lift its head. Both eyes were clear of Chaos's mark. "Your sister tells me that you speak of a past love of your mother's named Wil. She said to tell you to trust me. I served her when she was still a little bit Fomorii. She be a good girl. A kind girl."

The Fomorii lowered its head again. I wavered. There was no way it could have known what Ashling and I spoke of during our last dream encounter without her telling it. Damn.

Carnwennan went back into the scabbard. "All right. What do you propose?"

The Fomorii lifted its head, its tongue flicking out past the wicked sharp teeth its mouth barely contained. "I teach you, like I teach your sister. You need help. I give it. One lesson only."

Bres leaned in to me. *I know Gormley. I trust her. She has some strange abilities, but I think she might have something to offer.*

I lifted an eyebrow. "One lesson?"

Gormley ducked her head. She scratched a claw through the sand. "Yes, one lesson. Only one spell you need to know."

She backed away from us and I shook my head. "No, I'm not going with you. Teach me here or not at all."

A snap of her teeth and a kick of her feet in the sand preceded some heavy muttering. "Just like the sister. Stubborn."

Lifting her head along with one claw, she acquiesced. "Fine. I teach you here, but she might hear and then we are dead."

There was no need to say "her" name. We all knew Gormley meant Chaos. I would take that chance and I nodded for her to continue.

The Fomorii shuffled forward and I tensed as she lifted her claw-tipped hands into the air. "I need to be close to show you."

It took everything I had not to bolt or strike out as she came within inches. One claw touched Carnwennan. I glared at her.

"This is sword of power like Excalibur?" she asked.

"Yes."

"Then it has power to lift curse on the Fomorii," she whispered, her voice full of awe.

I hadn't thought of that. "I suppose it might."

She chuckled. "You are not surprised. You know of the curse."

It seemed best not to try to explain my near-death experience and the past battles I'd seen. "Yes, I know of it."

Gormley grunted. "Okay, I teach you one spell, one magic, and then you try to lift curse."

Shrugging, I agreed. "Trying is not the same as actually doing it."

"Yes, yes," she waved a claw in the air, "I understand. You are not Silver hand."

"She means Nuadha," Bres said. "The curse has been in force for so long, I didn't even know that he could break it." His violet eyes were drawn with worry.

What's wrong?

He shook his head. *Gormley is old. She was at the battle where the curse happened, and she hates Tuatha more than anything. This is out of character for her to help you. So while a part of me trusts her, still, be on your guard.*

I suppose desperate times call for desperate measures, I said.

Gormley lifted her hand again to touch Carnwennan. "So pretty." She tapped the gem with one claw. "Soul gem. It will capture souls if you know how to use it. That is your lesson."

I blinked. "That's it?"

She sat back on her haunches. "Yes, lesson I teach is that there is a spell to trap souls. I don't know it, but it's there still the same. Now you try to break the curse."

"Wait, give me a minute." I stepped back and

took Bres with me. "If I could trap Chaos's soul, that would free Ashling, wouldn't it?"

His eyes narrowed with thought. "I don't know, but it's a possibility."

Gormley snapped her claws. "Is not possibility, is truth. Now try to lift curse."

I shook my head. "That's not a lesson, which isn't a fair trade. You said you'd teach me something, not tell me something. That's a big difference."

The Fomorii growled. "Fine. I teach you first lesson. How to heal."

Bres was shaking his head. "She can't. It isn't in her, not those abilities."

She blew a messy raspberry at him, spittle flying through the air. "Stupid, you all are so stupid. There is always a way to heal, just what you are willing to give in order to make it happen." Scuttling forward, she put her face into mine. It took everything I had not to flinch from the razor sharp teeth.

"You are like your grandfather. You can heal, but every time you do, it will take a piece of your power. When no more power to take, it will take your mind until even that is gone," she said, her breath rank like old rotting compost.

"Back up, you stink," I said. Her eyes widened, and then she started to laugh, right in my face. Before I could react, her claws had gripped my head and she put her forehead to mine.

"Here, see what you must do to heal." Her magic hit me like a dark wave that rolled over me, tumbling me under the surf.

In my mind, I could see exactly how I would heal someone, drawing from the actual source of my power, giving that up in order to mend a body. Gormley let me go and I stumbled back, my legs tangling. I fell back onto my butt.

"That's not what happens to Ashling, is it?" Gods, I hoped not. I'd had her heal me twice. What if I'd caused her to be weaker, to be more susceptible to Chaos?

Gormley snorted and shook her head. "No, the other girl is a natural. First in many, many years. She heals like you kill, with no effort."

Her view of me and my abilities struck me hard. "I don't want to kill."

She shrugged. "But still, you do, you do and you do it well when others would die." Her black eyes bored into me. "Now, lift the curse."

I got to my feet and brushed off my pants. *Cora, a little help here would be fabulous.*

My mentor stirred within me. *You intend to try to break a curse that is thousands of years old, one that Balor has tried to break thousands of times over and failed? Arrogance will kill you yet, Quinn.*

"I'm not being arrogant," I snapped. "I'm going to try because I said I would."

Bres's eyebrows shot up. "You okay?" I waved him off. "Yeah, just trying to work things out as to how to try to do this."

Carnwennan came free from the scabbard with a soft, sliding snick. I held my breath as my mind raced. How was I even going to attempt this? Everything I'd done with my powers had been based on instinct and need. I neither needed this curse to be lifted, nor was I in dire straits, being forced to survive and dependent on magic that I didn't understand.

Closing my eyes, I thought about how Nuadha had held Excalibur high, how it had flashed bright, and then how the curse had taken hold.

The sound of the surf was deafening against the silence as I tried to see what I could do, tried to figure it out. Fomorii were creatures of water, and I, Lir's daughter, had stolen Card's power over the water. Maybe that would be enough. I opened my eyes and climbed the dune, then jogged out to the water's edge where the waves washed ashore.

With a quick thrust, I drove Carnwennan into the soft, wet sand, the waves spilling up around the blade. I kneeled in front of it in the surf and put my hands on the hilt, gripping the bone handle. I thought about my father, about how the powers he, Card, and I had were connected to all the water everywhere.

Fomorii were creatures of the water, born and raised with the ocean. All I could think of was how salt water was cleansing, how it could help a wound heal, and keep infection at bay. How water could wash away blood and dirt, and could leave you feeling clean. How water could take away filth and grime. How it could tear down even mountains given enough time.

Carnwennan began to glow and I let my power flow through the blade and into the water, through the ocean and through that connection to them into the people of the Fomorii. I could feel each of them, could sense their living force as if they each stood next to me, connected to the water as they were. Some, though, were afraid as they felt my touch through the power I used. They didn't want what I was offering. They didn't want what Gormley wanted.

I shifted the power a little and gave them the choice.

No one should be forced to do what they did not want. Like my mom shouldn't have been forced to bear children to men she didn't love. Like Ashling had been forced to give into Chaos. Like Luke had been pushed at me through a prophecy. My mind slid through these things and a truth settled on me, as clear as the night sky above.

Love and choices should always be freely given.

With that simple thought a bright burst of energy spilled out of Carnwennan. I held on, not realizing that I was screaming along with Gormley, who writhed in the waters beside us, her body contorting and twisting as the curse lifted, shattering.

With a final burst of light and power ripping out of me and through the water around me, I slumped over the sword, barely able to hang onto it. My body felt wrung out, twisted like a wet rag.

Bres put one of my arms over his shoulders and helped me to my feet. Without a word, he pulled Carnwennan from the surf and slid it back into my scabbard for me. "Thanks," I whispered.

My throat was sore. "Not sure I can lift it right now."

"We've got to go. Now." He was dragging me away, and though I tried to get my legs to work, there wasn't much I seemed able to do. A sob reached my ears. Someone was crying. "Where is Gormley?"

We half turned to see a wizened old woman, naked as the day she was born, sitting in the shallows. Her skin hung off in wrinkled folds, but she was smiling. "You did it. You are the Chosen One! This is the prophecy coming to light, bringing our worlds back together!" She wobbled to her feet and, the best her old body would allow, and she began to dance, sending up sprays of water as she kicked and hopped about in the surf.

There was shouting from Nuadha's camp, and it was getting closer. "We've got to go," Bres said again. "Gormley, you'd best hide yourself."

She spun to face us. "Never again, boy." Lifting one age-spotted hand, she waved to us. "If I die this night, I will die happy, and in my own body, the way I was born."

I lifted my hand, waving to her as Bres half-dragged me down the beach. I really was trying to move my legs, but they just didn't seem to get the message.

A snort and a splash off to our side made us spin around. Raising my hand, I prepped a power bolt. Or at least I tried to.

There was nothing left for me to use. I'd drained my powers. I looked anxiously for the source of the sound then hissed, "Bres, I can't feel my power anymore!" I didn't try to hide the panic filling me. How was I going to face Chaos without any way to defend myself?

"It happens to everyone, daughter." Lir strode out of the water, the two Aughisky at his side. "Only I suspect it is the first time for you. Breaking a curse that old and that powerful would have killed most, yet you handled it as if it were just another day."

In two strides, he was at my side, helping Bres carry me out into the water. "Hurry, Chaos has sent her army, and we are not in the best of shape to take her or them on," Lir said.

They helped me onto the back of the Aughisky, the same one that had brought me to the west coast. "Thank you," I whispered.

He grunted, tossing his mane. "If you can break one curse, maybe you can break another." There was a glint in his eyes that hadn't been there before. Hope.

Lir cleared his throat. "No time right now. We must hurry."

The Aughisky began to swim out into the ocean and within minutes, we were well past the breakers. Before I could protest, my legs were sucked hard against the Aughisky's side, like some sort of magnet had taken hold of them, and he dove under the waves.

Bres's words of warning whipped through my mind, but a light brightened beside me and I could see Bres on the other water horse with Lir swimming between us. Lir wouldn't let the Aughisky hurt me, of that I had no doubt. But then, the Aughisky had seemed inclined to keep me from hurt too, urging me off its back when it could have taken me out into the waves.

My mind eased on both those counts. I looked around us into the murky depths, trying to see where we were going.

We dove deep, the waters around us black, strange shapes flickering through our scope of light here and there. The water was cold, but it felt good on my skin. We started to slow as we came to a rock formation that was more than a little familiar, one that I never thought I'd see again. The entrance to the labyrinth rose up in front of us.

It seemed we were coming full circle. Bres dismounted from the Aughisky and I slid from the back of my mount with ease, floating in the water beside him.

Thank you. I mouthed. The water horse nodded, and butted his head against me.

Swimming was easier than walking, and I made my way to the labyrinth's entrance. Once more, Bres pulled me from the water and into the cavern that marked the beginning of the maze that I'd fought to get through to find Ashling. If only it had been that simple then to bring her home.

Holding me against his chest, he smiled down at me. "It seems we've been here before."

I held him tightly, feeling the strength of him steadying me. "I'm not letting go this time."

Lir cleared his throat drawing our eyes to him. "We don't have much time to make a plan." He beckoned to us to follow him. The walls of the labyrinth parted before him, the twists and turns disappearing as he walked as if he were Moses parting the red sea. Bres took my hand, linking his fingers with mine. Neither of us said anything, the memories of our time in the labyrinth swirling around us almost like flashes from an old movie reel. Of the fairy honey I'd tasted for the first time, of our first kiss and how he'd cared for me and my injuries.

This was where it had all started for him and me, where I'd found out that Ashling was Balor's daughter, where I'd faced my greatest fear. It seemed fitting to be back here now, at what I was sure was the end of the journey. One way or another, this would be it

"Can I save her?" I asked, the words blurting out of me before I even thought to stop them.

Lir paused and waited for us to catch up. His eyes were sad when he looked down at me. "I don't know, Quinn. I just don't know. Your mother spoke to me in a dream and said there was a way, but I am unsure of how true it was."

Darcy had said the same thing to me, that I could take on Chaos, that I was stronger than Ashling. But could that actually be?

"I have something to tell you," I said then paused, not sure exactly how to say that I had killed his son and stolen his powers. How did you tell your father you killed your brother? But I didn't have to say more than that.

"Card was no longer right in his mind. If you

wouldn't have killed him, he would have killed you, then me, stealing both of our powers, and in turn helping Chaos reign. You did what you had to," Lir said. His voice was monotone, flat, and emotionless.

"I tried not to," I said. "I tried to get him to stand with me, against her."

"I know. I felt your hesitation, and I felt his anger," he said, his voice softening. "There was no other choice."

I wanted to say more but even when I opened my mouth there were no words. Lir was right, there had been no choice.

While we walked the walls still dripped with moisture, there were no sounds of monsters in the dark. All the booby traps and dangers were wiped clean, now that the Fomorii were gone.

The throne room was as I remembered, minus the gaping pool of shark-infested water I'd had to swim across to get to Ashling. There was a throne with tables beside it set up on a dais, and a side alcove that held the tools and instruments for a scribe. The place for me was full of dark and unpleasant memories, it was not a place I would stay if I had a choice. It was funny to think that I'd seen it all before, yet hadn't truly seen it. My focus had been Ashling not my surroundings.

"We have to find a way to get you close to Chaos," Lir said. "I believe you can beat her, that you can end this destruction —but not if we can't get her to engage with you."

Bres walked to the one table in the room and pulled a map out of a cubbyhole I didn't even know was there. The two men started to discuss strategy and possibilities. They tried to draw me into the conversation, but I avoided it. My mind was wandering and, with it, my feet. Something drew me across the room and I followed the call of whatever it was that tugged at me.

There, tossed in the corner was an obsidian carved box, the lid half hanging off its hinge. Kneeling, I reached out and gingerly lifted the box. It was heavy, the weight of the stone making it sturdier than it looked at first. There were no carvings, no markings. Just a plain black box.

That was the box we put her in. It held Chaos for so many years.

I ran my finger over the lid. *Cora, please don't leave me now. I need you.*

I won't leave you, Quinn. This is the end game and I will stand with you now through it.

Tears trickled down my face. *I think I can kill Chaos and save Ashling, but...I'm afraid.*

Fear is a tool, one that often tells us what we are doing is the right path, that we are taking the route that we must go no matter how dark. The easy path is the one of least resistance, the one that is all light and goodness.

I trusted my instincts, trusted that what I was going to do and how I was going to do it. The men in my life would forgive me. Rising, with the box in one hand, I went to the scribe's desk. I sat down and looked at Bres and Lir. They bowed their heads as they tried to find a way to get me to Chaos.

What they didn't know was that I already had a way. But only *if* I was brave enough to see it through.

I took a breath. For Ashling, and for the one chance we both had I had to be brave enough, just one more time.

16

There in the throne room of the now gone Balor, the plans of how to deal with Chaos ranged back and forth.

Long into the next day, Bres, Lir, and I discussed how we would get close to Chaos—how they would get me close to Chaos. I took part in the conversations, so they wouldn't guess what I had in mind. If they knew what I was planning, they would try to stop me—and I couldn't have that happen. The one chance for Ashling's life depended on it.

"I still say that we meet her head on in battle, hiding Quinn at the back," Bres said. "We can move her forward as the battle progresses, rescue

Luke, and then both of us can flank her while she faces Chaos."

Lir shook his head. "It won't work. Chaos knows we have to get close and she will keep Luke by her side, using him as her shield."

It was growing late and I faked a yawn. "I need to sleep. I trust you two to decide the best course."

I kissed Bres goodnight, and then hugged Lir, hanging onto him for as long as I dared. Because this might be the last time I saw either of them. They went right back to their strategies. I watched them for a minute at the door, trying to take in everything they both were. Turning, I reached out for Cora.

Steady, Quinn. You are doing the right thing. They will understand one day. You have done well, my girl. Be brave now.

As quietly as I could, I made my way back through the straightaway that had once been the labyrinth. At the end, I slipped into the dark pool of water, feeling the cold settle into my bones. A head bobbed up beside me and my Aughisky stared at me, ears flicking back and forth as he narrowed his eyes.

"Where are you going?" he asked.

"For a swim," I whispered.

He snorted. "Hmm. A swim on the eve of a battle? Need a ride?"

I smiled and nodded. "Thanks, that would be helpful."

Slipping onto his back, my legs snapped to his sides once more with whatever magic he carried holding me tight to him. I still clung to him, grateful for the physical company on this last portion of my journey. Any tears I cried were swept away on the salty currents of the ocean as I said my goodbyes in my heart. I'd left letters behind in the black box that had once been Chaos's prison, but I still needed to let my heart grieve.

For Bres.

For Ashling.

For Luke.

Even for Darcy and the three Smiths. Don, Fianna, and strange old Gormley. Each had played a vital part in bringing me to this point.

Cora.

I am here. I will be here when it is your time to pass, Quinn. I will not leave you to cross over alone.

My heart clenched, then slowly the fear and pain faded. I'd made my decision. I knew Ashling would be angry, but that was better than the alternative.

Quicker than I had thought possible, we broke the surface and neared the shallows. Slipping from the Aughisky's back, I put my hand on his nose. "Thank you. I'm glad you didn't go back to the Smiths, that you are able to be free. No one should be chained."

He chuckled and pressed his nose to my shoulder. "Until they come to find us. This isn't the first time they've let us 'escape' for a time."

With a splash and a quick flip, the water horse disappeared under the waves once more and I was left alone treading water in the pre-dawn light. Swimming to shore, I went over my plan again, seeing it play out in my head.

There was still one part that might not work, one vital part. But I had no other option, and no other choice as far as I could see.

As I stood in the shallows, I pulled Carnwennan from the scabbard and spun it in my hand so the blue gem faced outward, then I slid the sword back into the sheath with care.

The world around me fuzzed as if I were looking through a gauzy curtain. I started to walk, keeping my steps deep enough that I didn't make any splash that would give me away to any who might be on watch.

Cora spoke to me as I walked. *Quinn, I did what I did, so the prophecy would be fulfilled. That is why your mother went along with bedding both Lir and Balor. She knew that you would need to be strong, so very strong, to face the evil that would rise.*

I thought about that a moment. *But, if she'd married Wil and had children with him, there would have been no need for us to be strong. Balor wouldn't have searched out Chaos to save Ashling. None of this would have happened. If she'd been allowed to love as her heart dictated, we would not be here now.*

No, you don't know that, she said, though I heard the doubt in her voice.

I backed off, not wanting to fight with her. *It doesn't really matter at this point. We must deal with this as it is. I'm not angry at you, Cora, just confused. And scared. I am scared that I won't be brave enough, or strong enough to see this through.*

She was silent after that, but I could feel her there. She didn't withdraw, and that was all I truly wanted: someone to stand with me in these last hours.

The Tuatha camp was visible from a distance, but the guards did nothing as I approached. They couldn't see me. I placed one hand on the hilt of Carnwennan, the bone warming under my fingertips. The smiths had made my blade true, and with the blue gem pointed outward, I was hidden from the eyes that would see me.

With great care, doing my best not to make a single splash, I made my way up onto the beach. My next concern was my footprints. Checking first one way then the other, I hurried up the sand, then pulled on the ocean, using the water to wash away the prints.

Good, that will buy you more time.

I wondered why Cora hadn't tried to talk me out of this. Of course, all along she'd been encouraging me to follow my instincts, to do what I felt was best, even when it meant jumping out of a helicopter. That memory hit me and I paused. I wanted to savor each moment of my life as best I could, now that it was near the end. That jump, that tangling of Bres's arms around me had been the start of so many things, not the least, my own growth.

Down the beach I went until I was at the camp that held Chaos within.

Working my way through the camp, I searched for Luke and Chaos. There was no doubt in my mind that Lir was right that she would keep Luke close as a bargaining chip, as a way to control me, threatening his life to offer up my own.

In no time, the sun had fully risen. It was hot, more so than any other summer I could remember.

It is Chaos's doing. She is slowly cooking the world, for nothing more than the sake of wreaking havoc. Cora said. *One of many things she will do if left to reign free.*

Sweat dripped down my face as I worked methodically through the camp, checking every tent for signs of Luke, hoping that maybe, *maybe* I'd luck out.

What I didn't expect to find was Darcy.

She was slumped in the corner of a small tent, sobbing. Her fingers clutched the silver ring I'd given her.

"Oh, Wil, I'm not a good woman, not anymore." Her fingers brushed against the polished metal as she spoke. "My babies are going to pay the price for my cowardice. If only I'd been as strong as them, if I'd fought back maybe things would have been different. I loved them so, and I threw them from me in a vain attempt to save them, if only they'd been your daughters, maybe this would be different." Her words echoed my earlier ones and I felt Cora retreat from the truth.

No, don't leave me! I said. I took one last look at my mother and stepped away from the tent, almost stumbling over Nuadha.

He brushed past me, the dark spot in his eye clearly visible. Pausing, he glared at my mother's tent. "Oracle, stop your sniveling. At least one of your daughters is worth the time you spent in a man's bed."

My fingers clenched and I fought not to take a swing at him. It would do me no favors to break my cover now, no matter the anger flooding me. But I knew where Nuadha went, Chaos would be near. As he left my mother's tent, I followed close on his heels, unwilling to lose sight of him.

He strode through the camp, barking orders, slapping people out of his way. At least I didn't have to worry about tripping over anyone else. Most people gave him wide berth, avoiding his reach and not even looking at him after he passed. Which meant my footsteps were going unnoticed.

At the edge of the camp, he halted and stared out across the beach. What had once been the Fomorii army now lay a mixture of humans and Fomorii as I'd known them.

You truly gave them the choice? Cora asked. *Why?*

Yes. I didn't want to steal what some felt was their heritage. Some have never known a body other than the monsters they were born as.

Nuadha yelled out. "My lady, I'd have a word with you."

This was it. My heart picked up speed, and my palms grew sweaty.

A green flag was raised, and Nuadha started out across the sand, with me close on his heels. As we passed the first line of Fomorii I realized that Gormley was there and she was looking straight at me. My blood chilled. Bres had said that the old Fomorii had strange abilities, but who knew one of them would be to see through the power of Carnwennan?

With a slow wink, she turned her back on me, more than that she did not raise the alarm.

Nuadha halted in front of a row of huge Fomorii guards, still in their monstrous forms. They slowly peeled away, revealing Chaos sitting on a throne studded with jewels and draped in fur as if the heat didn't bother her one bit. She wore a body suit of leather that was studded with small metal spikes along the arms and legs. Her hair had been shorn close to her head, bangs left to hang over her eyes.

Luke sat beside her, chains stretching from his neck and hands to the base of the throne. Other than being tied up, he didn't look as if he'd been hurt.

"What news have you of my . . . sister?" Chaos asked, her black eyes staring right past me.

Nuadha bowed at the waist. "She has gone to ground, or to water, it would seem. Other than that, we do not know."

She leaned forward, pulling Luke close by his neck chain. "And what of you, pretty boy? Hmm? Where do you think your precious beloved has gone with that handsome Fomorii warrior? Do you think he rides her one last time before I kill them both?"

Luke didn't answer. He just stared past her. She slapped him hard, drawing blood. I flinched, but he didn't. "Answer me or I will cut off that which matters most to a man of your looks." Her hand dropped to grab him between the legs. He stared stony faced into her eyes.

The silence stretched and just when I thought he would call her bluff, he spoke. "I have no idea where they might have gone. I wasn't privy to the plans. I was just told to stay here." His voice didn't give her one ounce of inflection, though his eyes looked pained as he stared up into her face. Maybe she hit harder than it looked.

"Hmm. I see," she murmured, letting him go so she could run her fingers over his face. "You are quite lovely. Perhaps I will keep you as the first of my harem. I would enjoy that. I think you might too."

His jaw tightened, as did mine. My hand inched toward Carnwennan, but I had to wait. I couldn't face Nuadha and Chaos. It had to be just me and her.

She flicked her hand at Nuadha. "Go, you are boring me." Nuadha saluted, and I stepped aside as he turned on his heel and strode away. Now, it was a matter of cutting Chaos out of the middle of all the Fomorii.

With everything I had, I tried to speak to Luke mind-to-mind. *I'm here.*

Luke's eyes widened, and then he started to cough, covering his shock well.

Try to get her away from the rest. Charm her.

He blinked several times. But he said nothing back to me, only gave a slight nod.

"Lady," he reached up and put his hand on her knee. "May I speak with you in private, away from all these ears? There is something I'd like to discuss. About Ashling."

I could feel the dose of charm he used even fifteen feet away. Chaos leaned into him, her hand stroking along his face. "Do you know how the gods caught me the first time?"

Oh, I had a bad feeling about this. *Draw back, Luke. This was a bad idea.*

Too late.

Her hand whipped around his throat and she started to squeeze. "They used a pretty boy to charm me into the trap. Very clever. I do so love a handsome man on my arm."

She tossed him backward and his body slammed into the ground, jerking against the chains as they pulled tightly. "My apologies," he coughed. "I didn't know. It's just... Ashling has been on my mind since I first met the two sisters, and I've dreamed of her most nights."

Chaos leaned forward. "Truly?" I tensed, wanting to know the answer too. And then it hit me.

Is that what Ashling had meant when she'd mentioned falling in love with someone? With Luke? Strangely, it didn't bother me the thought of her loving Luke.

He nodded, rubbing at his throat. They shared a long gaze, one that neither seemed willing to break.

"Hmm. Well. We shall see." She snapped her fingers and the Fomorii fell back, making a ring around the throne.

I had to push thoughts of Luke and Ashling back in order to focus. It was now or never.

With a single swift move, I pulled Carnwennan from the scabbard, a burst of light shattering the shadow veil I was hiding behind.

Chaos spun to me, her eyes widening. I pointed the weapon at her.

"Chaos, I have a deal for you. The sword that would be your death...for Luke's freedom."

The Fomorii lurched forward as I came into view, but stopped as Chaos raised her hand. "Wait, I believe the stupid twit means it. You'd trade a sword for his life?"

"Quinn, no! You can't do this!" Luke yelled, lunging as if he'd get between me and Chaos, the chains again pulling, stopping him.

She didn't step toward me. "Lay it on the ground and back away, and I will let your man go."

I didn't hesitate. I laid Carnwennan down, and backed off a good ten feet.

She waved her hand. "Farther."

I hope you're right about Carnwennan, Cora said. So did I.

Another ten feet and Chaos seemed satisfied.

"Well." Leaning toward Luke, she grabbed his face and kissed him with a deep, thorough kiss. "I suppose I'll never get my chance with you. Too bad, even the girl liked you. She kept you alive you know, what last little influence she has with me she made for you."

No doubt she meant Ashling.

With a flick of her wrist, the chains fell from Luke. He made as if to come to me.

"No, Luke, this isn't for you. You can't save me from this. It's my choice." I said. "Go."

He was shaking, anger and frustration written all over his face.

Chaos laughed. "Listen to her, or I will throw you back in chains, pretty boy."

And then I did something I'd never done before —I lied to him. *I'll be all right. Go get Bres and Lir. They are waiting for you in the labyrinth. They know what the plan is.* I knew he would believe me. I'd never given him a reason not to. His jaw was tight, but he left, running down the beach and diving into the water. It wouldn't give me much time.

"Now, I suppose it's just you and me, Chosen One," Chaos said, strolling toward Carnwennan. She didn't bend to pick it up, but flipped it up with her foot, catching the handle as the sword turned.

A few swipes through the air, then she threw the sword backward. "I cannot use a sword like that, not when I have my own. I think that I should like to share my story with you, before I kill you. Do you mind?" She lifted Ashling's perfectly arched brow at me, the jerky, marionette that she had been when she'd first taken over my sister's body was nowhere evident. She'd gotten better at using my sister's body as her own.

"Actually, I'd rather we just got to it," I said. This chatting business was not part of my plan. I knew I only had so much time before the cavalry showed up.

"Well, I'm feeling rather in a mood today." Chaos said. A crowd was starting to gather, Fomorii and Tuatha alike. Out the corner of my eye, I caught a glimpse of Darcy, her hands over her mouth. She may have had the mark, but she was still seeing her daughters face off in what was going to be a battle to the death.

Chaos strolled around me, circling me, within a foot of my reach. Close enough that with a weapon in her hand I would have been in trouble.

My jaw twitched. There was no time. I had to

do it now. I called Carnwennan to my hand, felt the smooth bone against my skin and swung toward Chaos. "I don't care about your story, but let me tell you mine."

A sword appeared in her hand, the same black sword I'd seen from my vision. The power that had caused the black tendrils to destroy the Fomorii made up her sword, the black smoke solidifying instantly into a razor-sharp blade. I had no doubt that one scratch from it would end my life. As we engaged, her eyes were wide with fury. "Kill her!" she screamed.

"No," Gormley shouted, holding her hand to stay the Fomorii. "We will not fight your battle." But not all listened.

The Fomorii ranks split, fighting one another. The Tuatha in the crowd swept into the battle, uncertainty obvious on their faces. Who did they fight? The age old enemy? Or each other?

Chaos and I we were at the center of it, our blades flashing bright and dark as we slashed at one another.

"My sister was the only person I had, and she was stolen from me," I said as our blades locked. We wrestled for control and I ended up shoving her backward. Not a graceful, skilled move, but it worked.

Pressing my advantage, I leapt toward her, a wicked downward thrust from Carnwennan skidding off the edge of her sword. That was not a move I knew.

Carnwennan has a mind of its own and knows how to fight. Let it guide you.

"I tried to save her, but failed." Tears prickled at the edge of my eyes. "But I won't fail this time."

Chaos's eyes widened, then narrowed. "You cannot save your sister."

"Watch me, bitch. Just watch me."

I spun in a half circle, Carnwennan whistling through the air. Chaos tried to avoid the blow but I shifted my balance at the last second, turning the slash into a thrust that took her through the stomach. The move left me wide open.

The world around us disappeared. Chaos screamed, rage turning her face into a twisted mask. The black sword arced through the air, slicing deep into my side. Like a bomb going off, pain exploded through me.

Steady, Quinn. It is almost done. Hold your place.

Shaking, my hands gripped Carnwennan, my

one palm over the stone that held Aednat's soul. "Take her," I whispered.

An image of Aednat flickered beside me for a moment. She smiled showing me her teeth, then disappeared. Finally, she had the satisfaction of watching me die. The power of a soul gem could trap a soul, and the soul that it would hold now would no longer be Aednat's, but Chaos's.

A bright swirl of blue and green light erupted from the blade's hilt and wrapped around Chaos.

"No, you can't do this!" she screamed her defiance. The soul gem started to hum and dark tendrils of mist seeped out of Ashling's body.

Chaos continued to thrash, her desire to live strong, but even she couldn't fight the pull of the gem.

"Ashling, fight. Fight for me!" I yelled, I let go of Carnwennan and grabbed her hands while blood poured out of me. I couldn't save us both. I chose Ashling, I chose her life to live for us both,

Her nails dug into my fingers as she yanked me off balance. We tumbled to the side, Chaos ending up on top of me, pinning me to the ground.

"If I'm going to be trapped, then I am taking you with me." She called her black sword to her hand, and I had nothing to block her with. In the back of my mind, I knew I could hit her with a blast of power, but I didn't want to hurt Ashling anymore than I had already.

As the blade came down, I braced myself for the final blow. "I love you, Ash."

She stopped in mid swing, a look of pain rippled across her face. "Quinn?" Beautiful, pristine green eyes widened as she slid off me, slumping onto the sand, her body shuddering once, and then going still. My mind skittered away from the possibility of failure. Not this time, this time I would save her. Clutching my own wound, I scrambled to her side.

I pulled Carnwennan out of her, the stone a deeper shade of green and blue, but otherwise unchanged. Chaos was trapped. "It's going to be okay, Ash. Trust me," I whispered.

My hand still had the etching of the cauldron on it.

Don's words came back to me. *"If you use the cauldron a second time, you will likely lose your life."*

"Likely?"

"Well, let's just say that it will take everything you have and then keep on taking."

Taking a deep breath, I laid it over Ashling's wound, her blood warm. I was dead either way.

The wound from Chaos's sword was on fire. The pain raced through me and making my heart thump erratically, dancing in every direction as though it would leap out of my chest.

Warmth spread through me as I willed what was left of the cauldron etched into my hand to heal her, pouring my powers from me through it and into her. Her skin flushed pink and began to knit together, the clean slice from Carnwennan closing over in a thin, white line.

Each moment that I pushed my energy into her, I grew weaker, my muscles going limp. I did not have much time to make this happen.

But Ashling still wasn't breathing. I used what Gormley had taught me, not to just try to use my powers, but to actually give them up. For Ashling, I would give it all up. It was the last thing I could do for her.

Everything I had went into those moments. First Card's power was taken, then I felt my own power begin to be drawn from me.

"Come on, Ash," I whispered. Her body jerked and her chest rose, once, twice.

"She's breathing!" I screamed, unable to believe that it was working, that I was able to heal her.

Gormley shuffled over to us. "There is only one problem."

I lifted my eyes to hers, but didn't take my hands from Ashling. The world around me was starting to tilt. The blood loss was too much.

"We do not want her as our leader," the old woman said. She lifted her hand, power swirling around her. I wasn't sure that I had anything left to stop her, but in this moment I could not fail. I cast everything I had into the fires that waited for me.

Ashling began to stir. It would have to be enough that she was breathing. It wouldn't matter if I healed her completely if I let the Fomorii kill her when she was still helpless.

Literally powerless, using the last of my physical strength, I leapt at Gormley, tackling her to the ground. The blast of power she released hit me square in the chest, throwing me backward through the air. Time seemed to slow. I saw Bres and Luke, running out of the water toward us, Lir close behind them. I saw Ashling sit up, a hand to her head. Her eyes were clear, bright and vibrant as new spring grass. A smile slid over my lips. I'd done it. I'd saved her.

A split second later I hit the throne, my back snapping with the impact. My bones crunched, splintering into pieces. I couldn't stop the scream that ripped out of me. The wound from Chaos's sword redoubled with the shock of so many things breaking at once. There was nothing but pain and fire and I could not escape it.

I am here, granddaughter. The pain will be but a moment.

I'd given Ashling everything to heal her. She would be okay. It was the only consolation I had. As I fell down into unconsciousness, my body giving up the last of its life.

18

Death, I'd been here before and it was not so bad. This time was different though. This time I felt more certain that there would be no going back. But through that came a stronger thought. I'd kept Ashling safe. The world was safe, but what was the world without my sister? Nothing.

I lifted my hand and shaded my eyes. Brilliant white light filled my vision and the sound of water on the sand, the soft shush of waves whispering in and out of the ocean rippled across the air. Blinking, I looked down to see that I was still in my khaki pants, tall boots, and white shirt, though the "white" could be taken into question. Blood splattered the middle of the shirt, my own for the most part.

My back didn't hurt from shattering against the throne, and the wound from Chaos's sword was gone, but I had a cut on my leg that bled all over the pristine beach, leaving a trail that was not being swept away by the water. That was strange.

I found my attention pulled away from the blood to look down the length of the beach. Across the sand came two figures, both I knew. The first didn't surprise me, her red hair floating on the wind. The other, though, shocked the hell out of me.

Balor.

He looked younger than when I'd known him, as if the weight of years and worry had been erased, and in that he looked a great deal like Bres.

They approached slowly, almost languidly, as if there were no hurry.

"Cora," I rushed forward and hugged her. "You're here. You didn't leave me."

She squeezed me back. "I'm so sorry, for everything, Quinn."

"Don't be. It's okay now. Ashling's all right," I said, meaning it. "I can let go knowing that I'd done what I had to do."

Balor reached over and took my hand. "You are an amazing woman, Quinn. I see why Bres loves you so. I am sorry that I could not see how simple it was for you, to love her beyond everything that others said would part you from her."

I blushed, not sure what to say, opting for a simple. "Thanks."

Cora took my other hand. "You will not be here long, my girl. Not long at all."

"What?" I whispered, confusion filling me. I was dead. This was where dead people went to be with their ancestors. I'd felt my heart stop beating, felt my body die.

"Why are you here?" I asked Balor. "Why did you come to me here?"

He shrugged, a soft smile lighting up his face. "To say goodbye, I think, and to tell you that you have done the things that no one else could, because of your heart," he answered.

Balor turned me to face the water. "What do you see out there in the waves?"

I squinted, the images dancing over the water, becoming clearer.

Ashling was bent over my body, her mouth open wide in a scream that I couldn't hear. Bres grabbed her, pulled her away from me, and put his fingers to my neck.

Then Ashling was there again, her hands on my face. She shook her head.

But what surprised me was Don. He was on the beach, and he had put one hand against my chest and one on my forehead.

Balor gently turned me back to face him. "I did you wrong. I judged you based on a skewed prophecy, instead of who you were, and more importantly who you are." He cupped my face. "Can you forgive me?"

I nodded, tears streaking down my cheeks. "Yes. But only because I know you did it for Ashling, because you love her too. Love makes us do crazy things."

He touched his forehead to mine. "That it does. Tell my children that I love them both, and perhaps that it made me do those crazy things." He let me go, then turned and walked away. I blinked and he was gone. All that was left were his footprints in the wet sand.

"I, too, need to ask forgiveness as well, and to say a final goodbye," Cora said, her hands turning me to face her now.

"No, you said you wouldn't leave me," I whispered. "I don't know you as my grandmother, but you *are* my friend."

She smiled. "Be safe, Quinn. Keep following your heart. It hasn't led you wrong, not once. Even when the path got dark and difficult, you were never wrong," She bent and kissed me on each cheek. "Tell Darcy," her voice caught and she put a hand to her lips, "tell her that I love her and I want her to be happy. And that I'm sorry."

The bright light burst all around me as Cora let me go. I reached for her, sobbing. She couldn't leave me now.

Light fading, I blinked, the blue sky above me all I could see for a moment. And then Ashling leaned over me, tears streaming down her face that dripped onto my own cheeks as if they were my tears.

"Hey," I said, my throat dry.

"Quinn, I thought you were gone!" She collapsed on me and I wrapped my arms around her.

It's okay now. It's all done. I said softly in her mind. *You saved me.*

"I didn't. It was him. He said you deserved a chance to live," She pointed to a slumped-over Don, his body motionless in death. One of his palms faced upward, showing the faded image of the cauldron etched into it, a smile on his face. I knew he hadn't been able to save his Mary, he'd been too late for her, but now he had saved me. I hoped that he was with her now, that they'd been reunited. I whispered a thank you to him.

"How did you know it would work?" Ash whispered in my ear. "How did you know you could break the spell and heal me and it would all work out okay?"

I let out a weak laugh and sat up. "I didn't. I didn't know anything of the sort."

Her eyelids fluttered and her mouth dropped open. "But then, why?"

"I couldn't do it, not even for the world could I be the one to take your life." I ran a hand over her head, brushing against her shorn hair. "And I trusted that you would fight for me as hard as I fought for you."

She burst into tears anew and buried her head into my shoulder. "I couldn't give up on you either. I just couldn't."

"Then why are you crying?" I asked, setting her back from me. "Chaos is gone, you're here, I'm here. What in the world could possibly be wrong?"

"What if something else happens?" she asked,

wiping the tears away. "Do you really think that will be the last evil the world will face? That we will have to deal with now that we are here, with the fae?"

I let out a sigh. "No, but I think we can take a break from it all, at least for the weekend. Don't you? Maybe we could go take those surf lessons. Someone did promise us a free lesson, didn't he? Bugger never did give us a single pointer."

We turned to look at Luke, whose eyebrows were in his hairline. He lifted his hands in mock surrender. "You're right, I did promise you lessons."

A hand on my shoulder turned my head. Bres smiled down at us. "You did it, Quinn." I put my hand over his.

"No, love saved the day, just the way it should."

19

The next week was a flurry of activity. Ashling retained her spot as leader of the Fomorii. Gormley had been killed by Bres after she'd tossed me into the throne and snapped my back.

It was a hard adjustment for all of those that were left standing after the battle. Ashling learning to lead and the Fomorii getting used to a leader who wasn't after power, but instead truly cared about their wellbeing.

Nuadha stepped down as leader of the Tuatha and Luke stepped into his rightful position. The council backed Luke completely, giving him the support he needed. He appointed Bres to the council, which both surprised and pleased me. They may not ever be fast friends, but they worked well together when they had a common goal.

Lir hadn't been able to rouse any of the old gods, so he'd decided to continue trying to wake them, to make them an active part of the world, to force them to help heal some of the damage that Chaos had caused. Though he'd forgiven me for killing my brother, he'd left shortly after with no promise to return. That had hurt. I'd thought for a brief time that I'd finally have some semblance of a family. Slowly, however, I realized that I already did. Ashling and the boys were all I needed.

I barely saw Luke that week. He spent many hours drafting up an accord with Ashling, one that would bind the Tuatha and Fomorii, and one that would allow them to come out to the humans. I still wasn't sure that was a good idea, but it wasn't up to me.

Of course, all that was after our surf lessons which were spent more in the water than on the boards. It had been a good day, our laughter chasing away the last of the darkness we'd faced. There were moments that I felt the urge to check the water below us, to see what might lurk, but a single touch from Bres would bring me back to the moment at hand.

I passed on Cora's message to Darcy, and she left to be with Wil. She'd cried and hugged me, then did the same for Ashling. Ashling forgave her without a second thought, as I knew she would. They promised to stay in touch. I did not, but I held no ill will for my mother. How could I knowing the truth?

The morning of the eighth day, Luke woke me early for a walk with him. I slipped into a calf length dress that floated on the ocean breeze and tied my hair into a loose bun.

"We haven't had a chance to talk all week," he said.

"I know, but you're busy and I don't really fit in here anymore." I said. "It's okay."

He frowned. "Don't say that."

I shrugged, bent, and picked up a sand dollar, turning the slightly fuzzy disc in my hand. "It's the truth. I burnt out my powers bringing Ashling back. I'm pretty much a human with some interesting genetics."

Silence hovered between us, awkward and uncomfortable. Nothing was the way I'd thought it was going to be. Every day that passed, I could feel him drawing farther away from me. It hurt, but deep down, I wasn't surprised. The council had released the original prophecy that Nuadha had suppressed. It said nothing about the Shining One being with the Chosen One. Only that there would be a union to bind the Fomorii and Tuatha together.

"The line of the snake will bring forth a saving light at the darkest hour. Binding all the realms as one—her sword will strike down the evil that haunts the land and the sword shall lead the fae to victory. Filled with compassion, the line of the snake's heart will remain pure and love will see them through. A union shall rise peace shall reign, and the world will know the fae for all that they are, and her sword will forever be at her side."

The thing was, I understood that prophecy clearly. Her sword . . .I was Ashling's sword. She was the one filled with compassion and love. The prophecy was about us both, and about the two us working together to survive and bring peace. There was no chosen one. Just the line of the snake making things right.

More than that, there was again no mention of the Shining One being with the Chosen One. Nothing at all about a union of that nature.

I think it rocked him, realizing that he didn't *have* to be with me. That it wasn't pre-ordained.

That what he'd started to feel for someone else was not only okay, but allowed. And that I knew it too. Because as much as I loved him, it wasn't the same thing I felt for Bres. Bres made my heart sing in ways that Luke never had.

Luke was family, and I loved him like a brother. Yes, I know we'd kissed, but so had Luke and Leia and they really were siblings.

Luke and I headed toward the water, taking advantage of the fact that the tide was out which gave us plenty of room. He walked with his hands in his pockets and I wrapped my arms around my middle.

"We need to talk about...things," Luke said. "I just don't know how to start."

I turned the dream I'd had the night before over in my mind. It came easily back to me and I saw it as clear as day. What I'd already begun to suspect was laid out in front of me.

Luke and Ashling were falling hard for each other.

Was this the start of my time as my mother's successor? To see what was coming for those I loved and cared deeply about?

Part of me wondered why letting him go didn't hurt me more. But I loved them both, and could see that he would make her happy, that he would treat her like the princess she was. Not to mention, the signs had been there when I looked back.

He'd started pulling away the moment she'd found him on the other side, when he'd been full of Aednat's banshee venom. He'd been pushing me aside as he'd fallen for her.

I held my hand out to him. "It's okay. I know about you and Ashling. I think I've known for awhile. The prophecy you've believed your whole life made it hard to see her though."

He blinked several times. "I do love you, but . . .not like that. You are family, Quinn."

"It's not like we were led to believe," I said. "I know. I know. But seriously, if you hurt her you understand you'll have me to deal with?"

He shook his head and laughed. "I hear you."

I thought about the moment that I'd been able to speak mind to mind with him, at the base of Chaos's throne.

Cora had told me, when I'd first met her, that to speak mind to mind required either shared blood or love. I did love Luke, just not the way that I loved Bres, but maybe it was more that he was important to me and he needed to hear me in those moments. Maybe the rules were bent just a little so we could survive and conquer Chaos one last time.

A tug across my shoulders, like the ghost of Cora tightening around me gave an affirmation to that thought. Yes, rules were made to be broken, even that one it would seem.

"I have to tell you, something happened, while I was floating between life and death. Ashling came to me, stayed by my side," he said, a frown creasing his brow. "She told me stories about her childhood, about her and you. I think that she was trying to tell me all the reasons that you were amazing, but all I could see were all the reasons that *she* was amazing." His frown deepened and I didn't understand why at first. "And then she kept coming to visit me, whenever I slept. One night, I got a glimpse of her most recent memories. With Card. Of him hurting her."

My jaw tightened, but before I could say anything, Luke went on. "All I could think about was how much I'd wished it had been me to finish him off, how much I wanted to protect Ashling and how much she needed me." He turned to face me. "You never really needed me, Quinn. I wanted you to, but you didn't ever need me. You just kept going your own way, and it worked. But I'm not the right one for you."

I smiled, though my heart ached a little, we both knew he was right. He'd wanted to be my white knight, and that had never been the case. Nor had I wanted it to be, not really. "If you hurt her, I will break you in half like a twig." I made snapping motion with my hands.

He laughed and the awkwardness between us dispelled on a gust of ocean air. Far down the beach, standing on the rocks, was Bres waiting for us. Luke nodded toward his at-times rival. "Besides," I said, "I don't think it's fair that I keep both of you. Seems a little selfish, don't you think to have two handsome fae men at my beck and call?"

Luke hugged me and kissed my forehead. "I guess I'd better get used to calling you sis then, huh?"

I smiled. "Yeah, though I should warn you that being part of the family is not all it's cracked up to be. We're a bit of a mess, crazy snake relatives, oracles, and grandpa back in a mental institute."

"I think I can manage." He let me go, turned and headed back the way we'd come, leaving me to continue on my own toward Bres.

My thoughts wandered to my grandfather, where this journey had all started just a short time before. He'd lost his mind over the years and when I looked back at my life I could see where he'd used his healing powers and slowly lost his mind in order to keep me and Ashling safe. A broken leg on Ashling falling from the tree house.

A head injury on me falling off a horse.

How many times had he used his ability to heal to get us to adulthood, and cost himself his own mind? "Grandpa, you shouldn't have." I whispered. Though I knew that he had done what he'd done for the same reason I'd done what I'd done.

Because he loved us.

Heading toward Bres, I thought of all that we'd been through, all that we'd seen and done. It was a lifetime of trust, love and adventure crammed into a short space of time. Which made it all the more precious. But I was worried that once the adrenaline faded, once the danger had passed he might change his mind. That he might realize he was better off with another Fomorii like him.

The council, all of them except for Bres, had insisted that I was not worthy of being bound to the Tuatha de Daanan leader without my powers. I didn't think that had anything to do with Luke's decision, but it worried me. Would it matter to Bres that I no longer had any abilities? That I was nothing more than a fae with no power in me?

Bres walked toward me. "Hello, beautiful, did I see you speaking to our mighty leader?" His mouth twitched and that sparkle in his eyes was back—the one that said he was ready to stir up some trouble.

"Only to let him know that if he hurt Ashling I would snap him like a twig," I said, trying to keep my tone light.

He spluttered, "Wait, what? He can't have you both! That do not be fair."

I laughed and bent at the waist, clutching my stomach. "Oh my God, Bres, he was telling me that he didn't love me, not like he thought he did. Ashling is the one he's fallen for, not me. It was like I thought, he followed me because he thought he had to, that the prophecy made it so. But he's being drawn to her, and vice versa. He can't fight it, nor do I think that either of them really want to fight what's happening between them." I found myself repeating the prophecy, the version that Aednat had known, the one that seemed to stick with me, the one the council had released.

"The line of the snake will bring forth a saving

light at the darkest hour. Binding all the realms as one. Her sword will strike down the evil that haunts the land and she shall lead the Fae to victory. Filled with power, her heart will remain pure. Through a union, peace shall reign and the world will know the Fae for all that they are, and her sword will forever be at her side."

I tossed the sand dollar I still held into the surf. "It makes sense." I told him my theory that the prophecy was about both Ashling and me, that in a way I was the sword, as was, Carnwennan that struck down Chaos, and all the Fae were victorious, not just the Tuatha. That the union doesn't say anything about the Chosen One and Shining One knocking boots.

Bres frowned. "Luke turning you away has nothing to do with you not being able to defend the realm? He's just got the hots for Ashling?" He frowned harder and I took his hand seeing the protectiveness in him rising.

"She's a grown up, she can decide who she loves," I said.

Twisting my hands into his, I gave a half shrug. "Does it matter if I don't have any power? Do you care that I am a useless human with great genetics now?"

He smiled and pulled me against his chest. "Not to me, it don't. My heart knew you from the beginning, and I'd have followed you whether you lead the fae or not, love," He kissed me, his lips sending little bursts of shivers through my body.

This was where I belonged, right here with Bres, a man who loved me no matter who I was or what I could do. Not because of a prophecy, or because I was strong or weak. Me, he just loved me and it was as simple as that to him. Suddenly I understood my mother's longing for Wil, to be loved for who you were, and not what you could do for people or the world.

As we walked along the edge of the shoreline, two familiar horse-shaped heads rose out of the water. Ears flicked toward us and I waved at them. "The smiths have not caught you yet?"

The Aughisky trotted out of the ocean, water spraying up around them as they moved toward us, tossing their slick black manes.

The one closest to me had been my mount, and he was the one who spoke.

"You saved the world from Chaos. We would be in your service, Lady of the Sea, if you'd have us. Perhaps one day you will find the way to break another curse."

"I am no one," I said. "I don't have any powers left. You'd be better off serving Ashling. Her and Luke that is."

They snorted and pawed at the sand. "We serve who we serve, and choose to carry you to whatever destination you will ride to next."

"You sure?"

The Aughisky bowed his head. "There are many journey's that wait, young oracle, do you not see what lies ahead of you?"

I blinked and saw Bres and I riding in an ocean that was not this one, but one near the true Emerald Isle. "Ireland." I said. "I see Ireland."

The water horse grimaced. "That is the place we would avoid, but it calls to us too."

I lifted my hands in mock surrender. "Then we have things to do, the four of us?"

Bowing with one knee, they lowered their heads. "Ride with us, Lady of the Sea, and Master of the Depths, and let us find a new adventure together."

Bres and I shared a look. "Race you to the far end of the beach," was all he said before we were leaping on the Aughisky backs, and galloping down the beach at a breakneck speed.

Wind whipped through my hair and stole the elastic, leaving my curls to trail out behind me.

Gripping the Aughisky with my legs, the motion of his gallop swelled through me.

The ocean called and I turned my head and held my hand out toward the water. There, just below the surface of my skin was a whisper, a faint touch of power I recognized, one that I thought I'd burnt out saving Ashling.

I swirled my fingers, and the water leapt toward Bres and his mount, slowing them down just enough that me and my water horse raced past them.

With a laugh, I called out over my shoulder, my eyes meeting Bres's, "I think I'm going to win after all."

UP NEXT!

Wondering what to read after this trilogy? Well, here's a couple suggestions!

For more Epic Fantasy Action Adventure check out:

A Court of Honey and Ash
(co-written with Kelly St. Clare)

(cover on next page)

For more Young adult style reads check out:
Shadowspell Academy: The Culling Trials

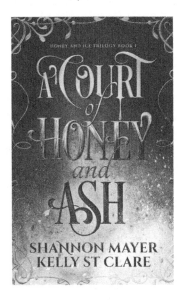

Orphaned. Trained to fight. Raised to fear the power of Underhill. Secretly in love with a man who doesn't want me.

I'm still just Alli, aka the half-human orphan fae, but my life is looking up for the first time. It only took me my whole 24 years.

But when Underhill—the ancestral home of the fae—shatters, making it impossible for any fae to enter, I'm the only one who knows who did it.

A secret that will be the death of me if I do nothing.

A brutal madness spreads through the fae as they lose their connection to Underhill, and to save my people, my only choice is to leave all I have fought for and go on the run.

Unless I figure out how the hell magic that has existed since the dawn of time was destroyed with a single touch, well, an entire life spent fighting to prove myself isn't going to mean anything at all.

I must find the answer to the riddle of Underhill's shattering.

Hunted by the very man I loved once upon a time.

If you love Jennifer L. Armentrout, Sarah J. Mass, Holly Black or Elise Kova, you will love this dive into a world of the fae, forbidden love, and a story that will leave you breathless for more.

ABOUT THE AUTHOR

Check out all my links to keep up to date, and my website for what's happening!

www.shannonmayer.com

Or Sign up for my newsletter

Newsletter Sign Up

Or check out my social media

Made in the USA
Monee, IL
02 April 2021

64528960R00144